A DEBT REPAID

A DEBT REPAID

PETER PRINSLOO

Published by Sunrise Script

A DEBT REPAID

A Sunrise Script book
First published in South Africa 2021
Copyright © Peter Prinsloo
All rights reserved

This book is a work of fiction and except in the case of historical fact, any resemblance to actual persons, living or dead, is entirely coincidental.

Sunrise Script
South Africa

Cover design by Deeper Blue www.wearedeeper.blue
ISBN: 978-1-9160819-5-6

1

Deafening noise shattered the stillness of the early morning, jerking the startled man from the waning after-effects of his drinking binge.

'Police, police, open this door, now!' bellowed a thunderous voice. The banging continued on the roof of the car, together with repeated threats to the man in the car. Louder still, dogs barked and growled aggressively. Struggling to focus and orientate himself to the developing chaos, the man stared up through blurry eyes from the passenger seat, only to be blinded by bright shafts of light cutting through the window. Sucking in as much air as he could, he attempted to right himself before collapsing onto his back with a stifled grunt.

A face pressed up against the driver's window. 'Don't lie down. Get up and unlock this door, now! If you don't, we're coming in.'

The bewildered man searchingly patted his naked torso, grappling to fathom the reason for his missing shirt. Nothing sprung to mind and nothing made sense, as a jackhammer pounded away in the back of his head.

'Right, that's it, I'm giving the order to smash the window,' shouted the commanding voice from outside.

Waves of nausea and panic swept rapidly over the prone man as he finally managed to lift himself enough to unlock the door before collapsing again. The shouting, barking and growling, as well as the brightness of what he could now see were flashlights, intensified the moment powerful hands grabbed hold of his arms and plucked him out of the car. The explosive jolt of the heavy landing on the cold concrete floor reverberated painfully up his spine.

'What's going on, what's happening?' came his muffled cry from beneath a knee pressed down forcefully on his neck.

'Pick him up and cuff him,' barked the now familiar voice to the officer pinning the man to the ground. 'And you, Sergeant Pillay, get the forensics team going straight away. I want this entire scene, including the car and everything in it, urgently processed.'

'Will do, Captain.'

'And where's that body bag? I want her moved when the pathologist's done.'

'I'll check, Captain.'

The captain turned and stepped towards his shaking prisoner, sandwiched uncomfortably between two burly detectives.

'I'm Detective Captain Kumalo from the Johannesburg Murder and Robbery Squad. What's your name and where you from?'

Confusion and disorientation reigned supreme, overwhelming the hesitant man. The few inches separating them weren't enough to shield him from the detective's garlicky breath. His eyes darted from side to side, taking in the frenetic activity as more people arrived and scurried about, some in police uniform, others in plain clothes. Floodlights were being hastily mounted on telescopic stands, and police barrier tape cordoned off the area around his car and a nearby stairwell. Then he caught a glimpse of two uniformed police officers rushing past, carrying an empty black body bag.

Kumalo took a step back. 'What's your damn name, and where you from?' he asked, more firmly this time.

'Jeremy Winters,' came the flat reply, his eyes continuing to flick around the drama that surrounded him. 'I'm a lawyer, what's going on?'

'What's being a lawyer got to do with anything?' barked Kumalo.

'I know my rights. You can't snatch me out of my car and throw me on the floor like some common criminal,' he protested.

'Where are you from and what are you doing here?' insisted Kumalo, stepping in close.

'I've been at my firm's party here at the hotel.'

'What's the firm's name?' asked Kumalo in a clipped tone.

Staring at the police officer, Jeremy replied in a slow deliberate cadence, 'Plaistowe Incorporated. You can't treat me like this; what the hell is going on?'

'Jeremy Winters, I'm arresting you on suspicion of rape and murder. You do not have to say or do anything. Anything you say or do can be used in evidence against you. Do you understand?'

'This is ridiculous. What do you mean "rape and murder"? Whose murder—when—where?'

'Do you understand my caution?' asked the detective sharply.

'I do, but I don't, don't under—understand wh-wh-why I'm a suspect. What do you mean? What's going on.'

Kumalo's eyes bore into him. 'My officers will take you to the holding cells in Hillbrow where you'll be held for at least the next forty-eight hours for questioning. We'll talk later.'

On his way to the escort car the dark reality of the moment engulfed him when he observed the officers returning with the body bag, now occupied. He stopped.

'Is that the victim?'

'That's a stupid question,' screamed the officer manhandling him from behind. 'You know full well it is, you raped and killed her, you arsehole.'

At that he was shoved forward and bundled into the rear seat of the unmarked car, without the usual courtesy of protecting his head. Even though the cuffs bit deeply, he stifled the urge to complain.

In between the waves of nausea, aggravated by the erratic high-speed journey to Hillbrow, he dredged the depths of his murky memory, desperately hoping to fill the void of the last five to six hours. Snatches of disconnected information darted in and out, causing more confusion. He remembered attending the lavish year-end office party in the Baobab Ballroom and drinking copious quantities of alcohol. Recollection of detail failed him. He vaguely recalled socialising with some of the other young lawyers and dancing with many of the female members of staff, although he couldn't at that moment figure out with whom exactly. He also recalled being quite drunk by the time the chairperson of the firm commenced his annual monologue, and thereafter heading out in search of his car, feeling queasy. As desperately as he tried, his memory receded into a vortex of nothingness, and refused to cooperate any further. *Perhaps when I've sobered up, I'll remember more; but there is no way I raped or murdered anyone. Why would I do that?*

Fifteen minutes later the car screeched to an abrupt halt in what looked like a derelict courtyard of a dilapidated building.

The dashboard clock blinked 4.06 a.m. One of his escorts flung open the rear door and roughly yanked him out by the scruff of his neck. 'Move your arse, you dirty pervert.'

Two officers pushed and pulled him quickly into the building, then down a long, poorly lit, dank passage to a poky cell that reeked of urine. The officers forced him to strip and put his clothes in a plastic evidence bag then threw some tattered clothing at him and left the cell. They killed the overhead light; the door slammed.

He lay on the cot but sleep evaded him. Counting sheep was an exercise in futility, as was his attempt at relaxing his body, shifting incrementally from the toes all the way up to the head. The stress of his arrest and the anxiety about a hibernating memory played havoc with his mind. The unbearable conditions added to his woes: the overpowering stink; the thin mattress on the freezing concrete floor; the scratchy blanket crawling with bugs; and the dirty clothing, many sizes too big.

He couldn't even hope that it was all a bad dream.

Life to that point had been perfect—a wonderful upbringing in a caring and loving home, a privileged private school education, followed by a gap year (actually more than a year) travelling the world and then five years at Stellenbosch University, before being recruited by Plaistowe's. And then this. *Did I hurt that girl? Did I kill her?* he wondered before screaming meaningless noise through the bars of his cage. Again, his inner thoughts hounded him. *Why can't I remember? What the hell is happening to me?*

The tiny bit of hope brought by the first sign of daybreak soon evaporated as he stared through tired eyes at the breakfast shoved into the feeding hatch. He couldn't bring himself to eat the cold slop served up under the guise of porridge or to drink the lukewarm chicory coffee from the stained mug.

Footsteps approached from down the passage. *Could this be the moment?* he wondered, quickly pulling himself up by the bars. *'Sorry, sir, we've made a terrible mistake. You're free to leave. Please accept our sincere apologies.'*

'C'mon, woman-killer,' screamed the officer at the top of his voice. 'The captain wants to see you now. You know the drill. Turn around and put your dirty murdering hands behind your back.'

As expected, the hungry cuffs once again bit painfully into his wrists.

'I swear you're going to pay for this, you pathetic weasel,' Jeremy muttered.

The old elevator clanked its way laboriously to the tenth floor where the officer pushed him into a windowless interview room. After unlocking one cuff, the officer secured it to the metal ring welded to a table in the middle of the room.

'Is this really necessary?' complained a wincing Jeremy.

'Shut up, you pervert. Captain's on his way.'

The door opened. Detective Captain Kumalo and Detective Sergeant Pillay entered. Although still queasy, Jeremy noticed, for the first time, Kumalo's confident gait and smooth appearance. He was a big man—probably in his late forties, perhaps early fifties, and slightly over 1.83 metres tall, strongly built, albeit slightly overweight—and smartly dressed in charcoal denim trousers, light blue shirt and fashionable sneakers sporting a white trim.

'Thank you, Constable Jansen, you may leave now,' said the captain dismissively.

Pillay crab-walked to another table close by, switched on a voice recorder and returned to his boss who was now sitting at the table with the cuffed prisoner. Pillay placed a glass of water in front of Jeremy, who took a sip.

'This interview is commencing at 8.30 a.m. on Sunday, 8 December 2019 and is being conducted by me, Detective Captain Kumalo, at the offices of the Johannesburg Murder and Robbery Squad in Hillbrow. Also present are Detective Sergeant Pillay and the suspect, Mr Jeremy Winters.'

Jeremy's attention shifted again to Kumalo's appearance. The shiny, cropped hair accentuated the perfectly straight parting, cut on the left side. Not a blemish nor a wrinkle could be seen on the closely shaved face. His fingernails had been immaculately clipped.

'Are you with us, Mr Winters?' snapped Kumalo.

'Yes, I am,' replied Jeremy curtly. 'I still don't know why I'm here. I'm innocent and someone's going to pay for this.'

'Mr Winters, before going any further, I must repeat my previous caution. You've been arrested on suspicion of raping and murdering Amanda Shelton in or near a stairwell between the fifth and sixth parking basements of the Egoli Hotel in Sandton City, sometime between 11 p.m. on Saturday, 7 December 2019 and 3 a.m. on Sunday the eighth. You're not obliged to say or do anything. If you do say or do anything, this may be used in evidence against you. You're entitled to have a lawyer present. If you don't have a lawyer or if you can't afford one, the State will arrange for a lawyer to be appointed to assist you. Do you understand, Mr Winters?'

Jeremy's lifeless eyes stared at the flaking wall, not quite believing what was happening.

'Do you understand, Mr Winters?'

'I do,' snapped Jeremy.

'Do you want a lawyer present?'

'No, what the hell for? I've done nothing wrong,' he said, getting louder.

Kumalo eased into the interview with some background questions, ascertaining Jeremy's age as thirty-five and that he became a partner at Plaistowe's two years previously, having been an associate in the mergers and acquisitions department following his training at the firm as a candidate attorney. Kumalo also learned that Jeremy was single and lived on his own in an apartment in Riverclub, a suburb not far from Sandton City. After a few more preliminary questions, the detective homed in on the real issues.

'How well did you know Amanda Shelton?'

Hesitation. It seemed unreal that he was talking about Amanda in the past tense, and yet he knew it was very real.

'She worked in our tax department as a paralegal, but I didn't know her beyond that. Our firm is large, with more than a thousand of us.'

'Did you at any time have any interaction or relationship with Miss Shelton?'

More hesitation.

'It's a simple question, Mr Winters.'

'I just can't believe this,' said Jeremy, shaking his head. 'No, I had no relationship with Miss Shelton. We used to greet each other in the corridors, and occasionally we interacted about work matters.'

'Are you sure, Mr Winters—no interaction at the party?'

He shifted in his seat, grimacing. 'This handcuff is hurting. Please could you take it off?'

Kumalo gestured to Pillay, who obliged. Jeremy rubbed the raw welts on his wrists.

'I don't want to see cuffs that tight again,' said Kumalo to Pillay. 'Make sure the rest of the team, especially Constable Jansen, understand this clearly.'

Pillay nodded.

'Now, where was I? Oh yes, did you not interact with Miss Shelton at the party?'

'Not in the way you seem to be implying. Certainly no more than with other female staff with whom I chatted casually or with whom I danced.'

'No flirting?'

'I'm not sure what you mean by flirting. I joked, chatted and danced with many women and it's quite possible that Amanda was one of them. Nothing more than that.'

'Why was your front passenger seat down?'

'You're not suggesting—'

Before he could finish, Kumalo cut in, his top lip twitching. 'I'm not suggesting anything. My question is simple. Why was the seat down?'

'As you saw, I needed to sleep. I drank far too much.'

'Why did you drink so much?'

'I guess that's what people do at parties and, besides, I celebrated the closing of a big deal.' He glanced at Pillay who sat quietly at the table scribbling on a note pad as his boss remained firmly in control of the interrogation.

'What time did you leave the party and who was with you?'

'I don't know. I remember feeling ill and extremely drunk and knew I needed to make it to my car. I guess it must have been somewhere between eleven thirty and midnight. I'm sorry to be vague but, as I said, I was drunk.'

'And who left with you?'

'I left on my own. There would've been no reason for anyone to leave with me.'

'Are you positive, Mr Winters?'

'Yes,' he replied quickly. 'As I said, there was no reason for anyone to leave with me.'

'Why did you have no shirt on when we found you?'

'I don't know. Maybe I took it off because I was too hot or perhaps I spilled booze on it, I can't remember.'

'Why, when we found you, was your car parked in such an odd spot?'

'What do you mean, an odd spot? I don't understand.'

'Your parking spot was isolated—far from other parking bays and elevators out of the way—in a dark, concealed corner.'

Jeremy's eyes flicked around the sparsely furnished room. The solitary overhead light bulb began to flicker noisily. He started to fidget, and tiny beads of sweat glistened on his forehead.

Kumalo leaned in, locking eyes with his suspect. 'Why are you sweating, Mr Winters? Are the questions becoming too hot to handle?'

Jeremy held Kumalo's stare, taking his time before racing through his response. 'If I'm sweating it's because I'm hungover, still drunk, and I've had nothing to eat and, no, your questions aren't too hot to handle. I've told you before, I've done nothing wrong and I've nothing to hide. I don't know why my car was parked where you found it. Maybe I moved it into a darker spot so I could sleep. I don't know.'

'Why was your trouser zip undone?'

'Was it? I had no idea, maybe I needed a pee.'

The detectives glanced at each other and, as if rehearsed, shook their heads in unison. Kumalo pressed on. 'Please explain to us, Mr Winters, how a pair of black panties found their way into your jacket pocket—the jacket we found on the back seat of your car?'

A protracted silence hung uncomfortably in the air.

'While you're thinking about that one,' said a smug Kumalo, 'also think about the scratch marks on your shoulders and down your chest and how they got there.'

Feeling faint and fighting the urge to vomit, Jeremy could offer no explanation because, so he said, he had no idea. The thought flashed through his mind that the panties may have been planted as a prank by one of his friends. *But what about the scratches?*

'I'm not feeling well, please can we take a break?'

'In a moment, Mr Winters, just a few more minutes.'

'My head is pounding, and I feel like vomiting,' he said, lifting the glass of water and draining its contents.

The light flickered noisily again. Kumalo glanced up and thumped the table, sending his pen to the floor and causing both Jeremy and Pillay to jump in their seats.

'This is damned annoying. Tell Jansen to get it fixed as soon as we're done.'

Without waiting for an acknowledgement, he resumed the interrogation. 'There's much you don't know. I find that strange. Here's what I think. You left the party with Miss Shelton and the two of you got frisky in your car. You moved the car to a more private spot, away from the elevators and other cars, and when Miss Shelton wouldn't have sex with you, you tried to force yourself on her. She jumped out of the car and you followed her into the nearby stairwell where you raped and killed her. You returned to your car where you passed out. Isn't that what happened, Mr Winters?'

'No!' he fired back. 'That's a bloody lie. I've never had a physical relationship with Miss Shelton, and even if I did I wouldn't have raped and killed her because she turned me down. That's just bullshit. That's not me, ask anyone who knows me, ask all the girls I've dated.'

Kumalo remained silent, locking eyes again with his suspect. 'Why are you so sure, Mr Winters? Your version is that you were drunk.'

'I would remember something like that if it had happened. Why would I possibly do this on my own doorstep? That would be stupid.'

'Miss Shelton was a beautiful young woman, and you couldn't accept her turning you down. I think you lost control, Mr Winters.' Kumalo paused again, rubbing his earlobe between thumb and index finger as he allowed his words to sink in. 'This interrogation is being terminated at 9.20 a.m. on Sunday 8 December 2019 and will resume in due course. Sergeant Pillay here will now take your fingerprints as well as a swab from the inside of your cheeks. By the way, don't underestimate our forensic tests.'

'These accusations are nonsense. I've never in my life forced myself on any woman and I never will. If Miss Shelton was raped and killed, the perpetrator is out there somewhere; it's sure as hell not me. I want to see my lawyer.'

'Sergeant Pillay will arrange for a visit as soon as possible,' instructed Kumalo.

'Thank you,' said Jeremy. 'Please could I be moved to a different cell? The one I'm in is freezing and stinks of piss.'

'All the cells are the same. Sergeant Pillay will ask your lawyer to bring in some warm clothes and perhaps a blanket or two.'

2

Barely a few hours had slipped by since his interview when Jeremy recognised the pronounced accent of Constable Jansen as he hurled abuse at another detainee down the passage. Instead of backing down, the prisoner stood his ground, delivering his own barrage of insults and challenging Jansen to step into his cell for a makeover.

'Maybe next time,' said Jansen, 'I'm on my way to fetch the rapist and woman-killer next door.' *Just as I thought*, pondered Jeremy, *a coward, through and through.*

Making his way noisily towards Jeremy's cell, Jansen didn't let up. 'Woman-killer, woman-killer, where are you?' he sang out.

Jeremy resisted the bait and waited at his cell gate, looking down the passage at the wall clock: 11.30 a.m.

'Don't think your lawyer is going to work a miracle here, Winters. He's waiting upstairs—a Mr *Fancy Smart Arse* Gary Edwards.'

The usual drill followed for the cuffing—deliberately tighter than necessary despite Kumalo's contrary command—before Jansen ushered him hurriedly to the interview room to meet with his lifelong friend and law partner.

'Hey, so good to see you,' he said, barely lifting his chin off his chest. His shoulders were slumped and his appearance disheveled. 'You have to get me out of this rotten place. They're accusing me of rape and murder. That's absolute horseshit. I can't take it, it's just too much.'

Stepping forward, Gary Edwards hugged him firmly. 'Please remove the cuffs, officer, and wait outside.'

'The cuffs stay,' said Jansen 'In fact, I'm going to cuff one hand to the table ring.'

Jeremy, although slight of build compared to the imposing constable, was fortified by the towering presence of his friend. He whirled around and shoved his face within inches of his tormentor. 'Now you listen to me, Jansen, and listen carefully,' he hissed through clenched teeth. 'Not only am I going to see to it that you are brought to book for the way you've treated me, but I'm going to sue you for every last cent you have. Now take off these cuffs so I can have a proper consultation with my lawyer, as is my right, otherwise the shit's going to hit the fan.'

Jansen retreated quickly, glaring at the prisoner, and then stepped forward with his fists balled. Before anything else could transpire Gary interposed his 1.94-metre, 100-kilogram frame between the two of them.

Gary, his height advantage over Jansen now apparent, quietly said, 'If you know what's good for you, officer, I suggest you comply.'

The cuffs came off and Jansen exited the room swiftly, grumbling, 'All lawyers are full of crap.'

'Thanks for getting here so quickly, pal,' said Jeremy. 'I need your help, more than you can imagine.'

'Thanks to Pillay for calling so soon,' replied Gary. 'He told me he and a Kumalo had just finished interviewing you. What the hell's going on?'

Beginning to shake, Jeremy's head collapsed onto his heaving chest as he battled to control his emotions.

'Hey, pal, take your time, we'll sort this out,' said Gary, placing his arm on his friend's shoulder and tousling his hair with the other hand. 'Here, I've brought some clean clothes, change into them, and then we'll talk. I also have a warm duvet and pillow, as well as an egg and bacon sandwich and some hot coffee.'

'Look at these disgusting clothes they've made me wear; they stink of piss, just like my cell.' He threw them off and kicked them into a corner of the room. 'I just can't believe it', he said, almost shouting, 'treating me like a common criminal. Who the hell do they think they are?'

After changing into the fresh clothes, Gary nudged him towards a chair. 'Take a seat and eat, you must be starving.'

He broke off a few small pieces of sandwich and tried to wash it down with the coffee, all the while scanning the room like a frightened animal. His hands trembled so badly that half the coffee spilled onto the floor.

'Slowly, slowly, take your time,' encouraged Gary. 'I'm in no rush.'

Marginally more composed after eating, Jeremy began to relay details of the suffocating nightmare since his arrest. 'This is beyond crazy, I had nothing to do with Amanda's rape or death. Why would I do something like that?' he pleaded for affirmation.

'You've known me just about my whole life, Gary, do you think I'm capable of doing that?'

'No, of course not, and that's why we'll sort this out. It might just take a bit of time. Why didn't you refuse to answer questions at the interview or at the least have me attend?'

'I guess that's the difference between acquisitions and mergers and criminal lawyering. Besides, it was just too early, I didn't want to disturb you after the late night and... I've done *nothing wrong*. I thought I could explain my innocence and be released.'

Gary moved closer, taking hold of his friend's shaking hands, squeezing gently. 'Stay calm, we'll get through this. You must be strong and keep a clear head. Run by me what exactly you told Kumalo and Pillay and what they said to you.'

Gary masked his grave concern on hearing the statements made to the police, saying, 'I hate to tell you this, but you and Amanda were all over each other last night—on and off the dance floor. The two of you couldn't get enough of each other.'

Jeremy stared, his eyes wide open and his head shaking in denial. 'Really? I just don't remember it that way. Didn't I dance with many other women?'

'No, mostly with Amanda. I kid you not, and many of the staff as well as some of our partners would have witnessed you two cosying up. When you left, visibly drunk, Amanda, also obviously drunk, left with you, clutching onto your arm. You had a bottle of champagne with you.'

'I can't believe what you're telling me. I have no recollection of that. My mind is an absolute blank.'

'That's what happened. How much did you have to drink?'

'Lots, mostly champagne, and I mean a lot. I closed that big deal late on Friday, you know the one I've been working on for months, and our party seemed just the place to let rip. And, besides, we always give it a bit of a go at the December parties.'

'Don't you have any recollection of yourself and Amanda at the party or leaving with her or of how you ended up flat on your passenger seat, with no shirt, unzipped trousers, scratches on your body and a pair of panties in your jacket pocket?'

'When you put it like that I know it looks bad, but I've no recollection. Nothing is coming back to me, and I'm frightened. What the hell has happened to me?' A pause filled the room with a prolonged uncomfortable silence before he asked, 'Do you think my meds together with the booze could've done this?'

'What meds?'

'I've been on a heavy dose of painkillers for about five days for a badly strained back—overdoing the golf a bit.'

'Could be. I know a mix of some meds and booze can be dangerous. You should know better, pal.'

'I know, I know, but I don't need a lecture now. You do believe me, don't you?'

'Of course I do, but, as you know, it doesn't matter what I think or believe. Did you tell Kumalo you couldn't remember? It's one thing to say you don't remember something and quite another thing to deny it happened.'

'No, I didn't; I denied things because I honestly believed they didn't happen.'

'You need to brace yourself, my friend, things don't look good.'

'What do you mean?' asked Jeremy.

'I'm meaning from a police standpoint. On top of the crime scene evidence, they're going to find out about how you and Amanda were at the party and that you left together.'

'So?'

'Jeremy, you're not concentrating. They're going to say you lied to them. And if the forensic tests show the panties came from Amanda and that traces of your skin were under her fingernails, they'll be even more confident.'

Jeremy suddenly felt weaker and even more nauseous. He dropped his face into his hands and sobbed uncontrollably. Gary manoeuvred his chair closer and again placed his arm around his friend's shoulders. 'I don't mean to frighten you,' he said, 'but just forewarning you of the road ahead. Hang in there, hang in there. I'll never believe you harmed Amanda in any way. We have a mountain to climb, but we'll get there.'

Gary walked across the room and leant against the door. 'It's not unheard of to have memory loss from binge drinking on top of meds, as seems to have happened here. But that's only the beginning. Someone killed that girl; either someone else from the party or someone from the hotel or even from outside, and we need to find that person.'

Jeremy jumped up and began pacing the room frantically, wringing his hands. 'I'm stuff... stuffed, every... everything seems to point... to point to me,' he stammered.

'Hey, get a grip. The truth will eventually come out, one way or another. It'll take time and you'll have to be patient. I'll do whatever I can to find the truth. For now, let's focus on your legal team, the bail application on Tuesday, and finding a psychiatrist.'

'What the hell do I need a psychiatrist for? I'm not mad!' said Jeremy, throwing his hands in the air.

'It's got nothing to do with your mental health, Jeremy, it's about blackouts from drinking. Your case is that you can't remember what happened because you were too drunk. The police are going to say you've lied about your memory. We need an expert witness to support you.'

'Sorry, Gary, I'm just a bit panicky right now. This is a nightmare from hell. You'll be on my legal team, won't you?'

'Not as your counsel. It would be unwise given our friendship and our business relationship, but I'll be in your corner to investigate the facts and to support you and your counsel all the way.'

'Thank you.' He stepped forward and hugged Gary. 'Please go and see my folks on your way home and let them know what's going on. Depending on how much bail costs, they should be able to cover it.'

'Will do. Any preferences for the legal team?'

'I don't know the court lawyers—I'll leave it up to you.'

'Okay, I'll get cracking and will see you tomorrow with some more food and coffee. Now listen... no, you're not listening, Jeremy. Focus. This is serious—no more statements to the police and don't let Jansen get under your skin. We'll deal with him later.'

'How do you know Pillay?' Jeremy asked.

'I've come across him a few times in the criminal courts and we often play league tennis against each other. I'm pleased he's on the police team because I trust him—he's a good guy.'

'And Kumalo?'

'Don't know him, but according to Pillay he doesn't like lawyers. I guess I'm going to have to watch him carefully.'

Gary banged twice on the door, announcing the end of the consultation. As the door flung open, he stared down at Jansen. 'Behave yourself, Jansen, or you'll come off second best, I promise you.' Jansen backed off, throwing a furtive glance towards Jeremy.

'I'll be watching you, Jansen,' growled Gary, looking over his shoulder as he left. 'Let me know if he gives you any trouble,' he shouted back to Jeremy.

As the elevator door opened, he heard Pillay calling from behind. 'Just the man I want to see.'

'Hey, Dhanraj, what's up?'

Pillay steered Gary into an office leading off the passage.

'We're taking swabs for DNA analysis, initially from all the young guys who attended the party. Seeing you're here, let's get you done, if you don't mind.'

'I don't mind at all. Comforting to see you getting on with things so quickly.'

3

With the top down, Gary's 1973 Ferrari Dino purred quietly along the leafy suburban avenue towards home, attracting admiring stares from some of the joggers, cyclists and strolling families taking advantage of another cloudless summer's day. It hadn't been his usual Sunday morning. He had struggled to shake off the forlorn image of Jeremy's elderly parents when they heard the news of their son's incarceration.

Gary was glad to get home. As he fiddled awkwardly with the uncooperative door key, his staffie barked excitedly on the other side of the door, scratching at the barrier between them.

'Hey Charlie, be patient, boy, I'm coming, I'm coming.'

The dog became even more excited, barking louder and scratching faster.

The phone in his pocket rang, probably for the fifteenth time since his visit to Jeremy. News of Amanda's death had spread quickly, with calls coming in from as far as Australia, New Zealand, the United Kingdom, Zimbabwe and Portugal.

'No, that's not so. Yes, the police have arrested Jeremy, and no, he did not rape or kill Amanda. We're on top of it. No, I can't spend time now, I'm running around. I'm about to fire off a group message to everyone at the office. Okay, bye.'

The door from the garage into the house flew open and Charlie came bounding through. Gary knelt and swept Charlie into his arms, allowing his powerfully built pet to slobber into his neck, grunting excitedly.

'Okay, okay, Charlie, I'm also happy to see you—come now, calm down.'

Gary hunted in his jacket pocket and immediately Charlie sat on his haunches knowing exactly what was coming. He cocked his ears and turned his head at an angle, looking up with large brown eyes, waiting for the treat.

Once the dog settled, Gary set his mind to the task at hand. Tuesday loomed and much needed to be done in preparation for Jeremy's bail application. Continued custody beyond that date was, as anyone familiar with Johannesburg prisons would know, a thought too horrid to contemplate. Gary wolfed down a cold snack before calling a trusted colleague from another law firm as well as two criminal law advocates from the Johannesburg bar to arrange for an urgent meeting the following morning.

That done, it was time for damage control—an email on the firm's intranet to all partners and staff.

Dear Colleagues

I'm sending you this note in my personal capacity as Jeremy Winters' closest friend. He joins me in extending our heartfelt condolences and sympathies to

Amanda's family and friends on her untimely, sad, and tragic passing.

I'm sure you must be as shocked and horrified as we are.

Rumours are rife and fraught with wild speculation. I've met with Jeremy and I've spoken to the police. They believe Amanda was attacked in the parking basement of the Egoli Hotel and they've detained Jeremy for questioning because he was found asleep in his car in the immediate vicinity of the stairwell where Amanda's body was located.

Gary omitted any further detail.

The investigation is in its infancy and therefore it would be premature and certainly most improper to draw any conclusions at this stage.

I have known Jeremy just about his whole life. Many of you also know him well. I refuse to believe he had any hand in this tragic and despicable event. I ask of you two things. Please don't gossip or speculate as this will be disrespectful to everyone concerned, and, if any one of you has any information that may help to find out who was responsible, please contact me or, if you prefer, Detective Sergeant Pillay at the Johannesburg Murder and Robbery Squad.

For obvious reasons, we cannot represent Jeremy, so an outside legal team has been engaged.

Gary Edwards

Within minutes, David Plaistowe, the chairperson of the firm, called.

No greeting, no expression of sympathy. 'Who gave you the right to engage with the police or with the entire staff?' he yelled, apparently apoplectic with rage. 'This is a firm matter and as such it should be handled by the managing partners.'

'Whoa, David, with respect—'

Before Gary could continue, David cut in at the top of his voice.

'Don't you "whoa" me, young man. Who do you think you are? This is serious and needs to be handled carefully. We cannot afford another public scandal.'

'As Jeremy's lifelong friend and business partner, I'm trying to be supportive,' he said as calmly as he could, fighting the urge to react more emphatically.

'Well what matters to me right now is the well-being of Plaistowe Incorporated and avoiding a mass exodus of clients. I've called a managing partners' meeting for ten o'clock tomorrow morning. Make sure you're there. And no more communications with partners, staff, police, or anyone else for that matter until we meet tomorrow. Understood?'

'I'll see you tomorrow, David,' replied Gary coolly. He terminated the call and slid the phone across the table, annoyed by his boss's admonishment.

The following day a sombre mood permeated the air as Gary made his way down the lengthy passage, flanked by lawyer offices on one side and support staff cubicles on the other. He sensed his every step was being closely observed, the usual chatter and laughter at the start of the working day eerily absent.

Before he could unpack his briefcase, colleagues began popping into his office wanting to know more about Jeremy's predicament. He turned them away politely with the stock answer that he couldn't discuss the matter pending his meeting with the managing partners. Those that cared about Jeremy registered their genuine disappointment at not being able to engage; the rest simply drifted off, no doubt hoping for the juicy gossip later.

However, one colleague's demeanour differed remarkably from the rest. He swaggered in to Gary's half-full office, not bothering to greet him or ask after Jeremy. The man leaned against the wall behind the others.

'So, what makes you think he didn't do it?' asked Roger Plaistowe, hands on hips and a Mont Blanc pen clenched between his teeth.

'I beg your pardon,' said Gary with forced formality.

The small group stood aside, which left the chairperson's son facing him.

'You seem pretty certain your mate had nothing to do with Amanda's death. Why are you so certain?' asked Roger.

'You're being insensitive and bloody provocative, Roger, get out, get out of my office.'

He took a threatening step towards Gary and pulled the pen from his mouth, pointing it at Gary's face. 'I'm not the insensitive one here. The blue-eyed hotshot isn't as wonderful as everyone thinks he is.'

'Get that pen out of my face and get out of my office,' said Gary, glaring.

'Don't tell me what to do. You don't know how lucky you are to have a position here at Plaistowe's.'

'I'm asking you for the last time, please leave my office,' replied Gary, more firmly.

Instead of removing himself, Roger continued waving the pen close to Gary's nose.

'I never trusted your mate,' said Roger. 'I for one am not surprised to hear what he did to poor Amanda. I think—'

Before he could utter another word, Gary slapped the pen out of Roger's hand, at the same time smashing his huge fist into the smirking face, flooring him. Undeterred by the spurting blood, he bent over the sprawled figure and swept him up in one effortless move. Buttons flew off the bloodied shirt as Gary yanked Roger's limp body towards him until their faces were no more than an inch apart.

'You little jerk, how dare you—how *dare* you? You've always been insanely jealous of Jeremy because he, and not you, is the rising star in the firm, despite your father being the chairperson. If ever you accuse my friend again, you'll rue the day you were born. Now get the hell out of my office you rotten pile of garbage.'

Roger skulked off, clutching at his nose, trying to staunch the blood oozing through his fingers. He shouted, 'You'll pay for this, Edwards, you're going to pay.'

The onlookers slipped back to their workstations, some applauding with silent gestures, and others not shying away from vocal approval. Few people at the firm liked Roger. Most detested the rude son and heir because of his arrogance and sense of entitlement, too much like his father, they thought.

Gary noticed he was splattered with blood, so quickly changed into a spare shirt. He examined his tender right hand. *What the hell have I done? So bloody unprofessional*, he chided himself.

'Let me look at that,' whispered his personal assistant, cautiously peeking around the door.

'Thanks, Lucy, I'll be fine, but would love a cup of coffee if you're offering.'

He brooded, sipping his coffee while half listening to Lucy.

'This is terrible,' she said. 'I can't believe it. Amanda and I shopped together on Saturday morning for our party dresses. Poor girl, I was fond of her. I also know that Jeremy could never have done this. Sorry, Gary, I'm prattling on a bit. Is there anything else?'

'Nope, thank you. I better get going.'

On his arrival at the top floor he found everyone seated in the opulent meeting room reserved for the exclusive use of the chairperson and managing partners. No doubt they had already met over an impromptu breakfast, the remains of which were scattered on the table. Conversation stopped as he entered, and their body language reflected an unfamiliar coldness and hostility, something he had never felt at the firm. He had always been popular and well-liked and feedback at his annual reviews indicated that he was going places, not only in the profession, but also within Plaistowe Incorporated. There had recently even been talk of him being invited onto the Managing Partners' Committee to represent the young blood.

'Take a seat,' came the first frosty words from David Plaistowe.

Plaistowe was an immensely powerful and influential figure, both within and outside the firm, and he knew it. Gary had always nurtured a professional respect for him, even personal regard. But this was a new Plaistowe, one who was circling the wagons. He sat back in his seat at the head of the table.

Gary said nothing, hoping for a greeting or a little regret over Amanda's death or sympathy for Jeremy's predicament. Nothing. Gary, having no intention of behaving in the same manner, greeted all the partners courteously.

'According to your email you've met with Jeremy and spoken to the police,' said Plaistowe. 'Tell us exactly how this came about and what transpired.'

Gary rested his interlocked hands on the polished rosewood table, making occasional brief eye contact with the glaring stares. 'I first became aware of the incident when Detective Sergeant Pillay phoned me at about nine thirty yesterday morning. He said Jeremy had been detained on suspicion of rape and murder and that he had asked to see me. Pillay suggested I bring a change of clothes, some bedding and food as Jeremy was to remain in detention pending his bail hearing on Tuesday morning.'

He paused, conscious of the silence and unblinking stares, and then continued. 'I know Pillay well and pushed for more information. He said Amanda had been murdered in a parking basement stairwell late on Saturday night or in the early hours of Sunday morning, and appeared to have been raped, and that Jeremy had been detained because he was found asleep in his car parked in the immediate vicinity.'

'Is that all the police told you?' asked Plaistowe, raising his bushy eyebrows and staring down a zipline nose at Gary.

'Other than to say that investigations were ongoing, that's all.'

'And what about Jeremy, what did he have to say?' The eyebrows now formed exaggerated arches.

'As you can no doubt appreciate, my friend, and *our* partner—I repeat, *our* partner—was distraught, bewildered and confused when we met. He wasn't able to tell me much other than to say he was drunk when he left the party and that he had no recollection of anyone leaving with him or of anything else until woken up by the police.'

'Drunk—by golly, that's a gross understatement if ever I've heard one,' interjected Sebastian Bagley-Smith, the head of the firm's lucrative tax practice, and one of Plaistowe's favourite lieutenants.

Ignoring the rude interjection, Gary raised his voice, and said with deliberate slowness, 'He denies raping Amanda or having anything to do with her death. I believe him.'

Plaistowe leaned forward in Gary's direction, pushing the palms of his hands down on the table and adopting the grave expression for which he was well known. 'Of course you do,' he said with a sarcastic edge. 'Did you not see how he and Amanda behaved at the party? My goodness. All of us there saw the two of them. And by the way, I, and many others, also noticed them leaving together.'

'What are you implying, David?' snapped Gary, struggling to retain his composure.

'Don't raise your voice at me, young man; you'll treat me with respect.'

'I don't mean any disrespect, but I'm not going to sit here and ignore ugly innuendos about my friend and—shall I say it again—*our* partner. Jeremy cosying up to Amanda and vice versa does not equal rape or murder; any decent lawyer knows that!'

'If you keep that tone with me, you are sailing close to a disciplinary.'

Gary took a deep breath.

Plaistowe continued. 'You have to admit that the circumstantial evidence doesn't paint a pretty picture. Be that as it may, all will come out in due course, I'm sure.'

Gary couldn't avoid affecting an expression of disappointment. 'I'm confident Jeremy will be proved innocent,' he said, 'but meanwhile we should give him our support.'

There were meaningful glances around the table. Plaistowe seemed to notice the mood of impatience around the table.

'Your note mentioned that an outside legal team had been engaged,' he said. 'Why so soon and why without consulting us?'

'Jeremy asked me, as his friend and in no other capacity, to arrange this for him urgently. It's his prerogative alone to choose his legal team.'

'I take it then that you will no longer be involved?' said Plaistowe, leaning back with an air of satisfaction.

'I won't be lawyering if that's what you're asking, but of course I'll support him as my friend, and I'll help out on investigations to prove his innocence.'

The deputy chairperson, Susanne Kuhn, another favoured lieutenant, butted in. 'You can't become involved in any aspect of the matter, Gary, and that includes investigations.'

'Why not?'

'Because you're a partner of this firm and after the last scandal we cannot possibly be seen to be taking sides. Our clients will ditch us and not come back this time.'

'Is that how all of you feel?' Gary asked, looking at each of the partners in turn.

Bagley-Smith languidly dabbed away croissant crumbs from the corners of his mouth. In an affected English accent, he said, 'Edwards, we cannot afford another scandal.'

Gary noted the sneering use of his surname. He searched the partners' expressions but all he saw was a tacit consensus with Bagley-Smith's assessment.

'We owe it to our employees,' said another partner.

'The clients will pack their bags before you can say "boo",' offered a third, and so on, and so on.

An uncomfortable silence swallowed the room. All eyes were on Gary Edwards.

'I'm afraid I won't—I can't—abandon my friend in his time of need,' he said.

'Do you really want to risk losing everything you have here at Plaistowe's—prestige, high earnings—considerably more than anywhere else in the country—enviable client base, and so much more?' asked Plaistowe.

'Are you threatening me, David?'

'Let me put it this way, this firm will not run the risk of another scandal, and by you, as a partner of this firm, actively associating yourself with Jeremy during this time, exposes us to risk. I won't have it.'

'My sentiments exactly,' said Bagley-Smith, with a soft clapping of his hands. The others nodded their heads in agreement.

Gary suspected this moment might come and had spent the best part of the previous night reflecting on the potential for considerable personal cost to him of being loyal to his friend. For years he had lived the good life in the fast lane and enjoyed the trappings of success—his Ferrari and magnificent home in one of the city's sought after estates, the exotic holidays, and much more. Could he give it up? It would be painful, and could take years, many years, if ever, to claw his way back to these lofty heights. He was also mindful of another looming financial pressure because of his father's deteriorating illness and his parents' meagre resources. But he had no choice; he owed Jeremy and the rest of the Winters family, and he would simply have to make a plan when his parents needed money, even if it meant taking out a second mortgage on his home.

'I guess that leaves me with no option,' he said, looking first at Plaistowe and then at each of the others. 'My two associates are fully up to speed with my cases and will have no difficulty briefing another partner to take over. My resignation will be on your desk within the hour, David. I'll let my clients know to expect urgent contact from you or another partner.' He stood, pushing his chair back noisily before heading for the door. He looked back. 'I'm disappointed in all of you. You're nothing but a bunch of gutless cowards. And one more thing: I've seen how some of you in this room behave at firm functions and you have the temerity to cast the first stone. You disgust me.'

Plaistowe jumped up, attempting to cut in, but Gary turned his back and left the room.

Some close colleagues congregated in Gary's office on his return. Lucy noticed his ominous expression. 'Are you okay?' she asked. 'Is there anything we can do to help?'

'Thank you, but not for the moment. I've resigned. I'm going because the managing partners want me to have nothing to do with the investigation. I'm sorry, I can't abandon my mate, so I'm out of here.'

'Oh no!' came a collective response from the small crowd that now formed in his office, followed by some individual reactions.

'What a bunch of shits. How can they do that?'

'That's not fair. What's happened to "innocent until proved guilty"?'

'Perhaps all of us, and Jeremy's other friends, should also resign.'

'Slow down, guys, no need to overreact,' said Gary, catching Lucy's saddened expression. *Were her eyes watering?*

She turned away and took a tissue from her sleeve. She cleared her throat before turning back. 'Gary, isn't this a bit drastic? You guys must be very close for you to put everything on the line for Jeremy.'

'You could say that,' he replied, leaving something important unsaid.

He turned back to address the room. 'Although it irks me, I can, sort of, understand where they're coming from. Let's not overlook the near catastrophic fallout a couple of years back when the firm stood by Swanepoel.'

'I wasn't here. What happened?' asked a colleague.

'Swanepoel, a partner in the family law department, had a sexual relationship, a consensual one I might add, with the adolescent daughter of a client represented by him in a custody battle. The client was the CEO of the firm's largest corporate customer.'

'Oh dear,' uttered a voice in the crowd, 'that was beyond stupid.'

'The firm stood by a guilty man and paid the price, literally. It cost the firm dear. Anyway, I'm sure Jeremy will be most touched by your support and loyalty, but don't rush things,' cautioned Gary. 'The truth will come out. Sure, Jeremy was bombed and sure, he and Amanda were getting it on, but he would never do anything like this. However, there is something you guys can do, but discretion is called for. David Plaistowe is not someone to be toyed with. His tentacles reach far, and he can be a vindictive bastard.

I've seen another side to him today. Keep your eyes and ears open for anything that may help Jeremy and let me know.'

'What happens to Jeremy in the meanwhile?' asked another friend in the group.

'I'm quite sure he'll be released on bail on Tuesday, but I also have no doubt the firm will place him on garden leave.'

'Won't the police oppose bail until their investigations are done?'

'They might, I guess, but I can't see them winning that one,' said Gary. 'There's nothing to suggest he's a flight risk—quite the opposite I would suggest—or that he will hamper their investigations in any way.'

4

As Gary hoped and expected, the bail application succeeded. The magistrate ordered Jeremy's release on payment of R250,000 bail, the surrender of his passport, and that he be fitted with an electronic bracelet.

'In addition,' said His Worship, 'you are to report to the Sandton Police Station every day at 10 a.m. If you don't, or if you tamper with the bracelet, you will be arrested, returned to custody and your bail will in all probability be estreated. Do you understand?'

'I do, Your Worship.'

'Good. The court will adjourn for ten minutes.'

Jeremy turned slowly, a broad smile breaking across his handsome, boyish face. Mr and Mrs Winters rushed over and hugged him before Gary joined them, taking his friend's extended hand.

'Thanks for organising things, pal,' Jeremy whispered. 'I'll call you later today. I'm moving out of my apartment and going to stay at my folks' place,' he announced, glancing at them, 'if they'll have me.' They hugged him again.

'Besides a decent shower, I think you need some good old home comforts,' replied Gary, patting Jeremy on the shoulder.

Descending the steps outside the court building, Gary checked his phone and noticed missed calls from Lucy and two of his friends at Plaistowe's. He also had three voice messages. Two were rather flattering invitations from colleagues at other law firms, keen to talk to him about his future. The third was from a journalist at *The Chronicle*, asking him to call back.

He then selected the missed call from Lucy. 'Hi, what's up?'

'How did it go?' she asked.

'As expected. Jeremy should be out within the hour.'

'Great. Please send him my best wishes. The other reason for wanting to chat is to bring you up to speed on what's happening here at the firm. David Plaistowe has written to everyone warning them, under threat of disciplinary action, not to involve themselves in the case in any way, unless approached by the police. I'll forward you a copy of his note. You'll see he also mentions your resignation; nothing derogatory but merely saying that because of your close friendship with Jeremy and your intention to help him, it would've been inappropriate for you to continue being a partner.'

'Interesting, but hey, I'm not going to lose any sleep about resigning. *At least I hope not.* There are opportunities out there, I'll probably have to cut back somewhat, though.'

'That brings me to something else I've been wanting to say. No doubt you'll be looking for a position at another practice. If you'll have me, I'd like to continue working with you wherever you land up.'

He valued Lucy, having taken her on some years back as a junior legal secretary straight from secretarial college. He was particularly impressed that she had, before college, attended university, graduating with a bachelor's degree in business administration. She soon made her mark and after a couple of years became his personal assistant.

'Of course, Lucy, thank you. I was going to ask you the same thing. Stay put for the moment and keep it to yourself. I'll update you as things move forward. I'm not sure how long it'll be before I take up another position.'

'Understood,' said Lucy.

'How are the staff reacting?'

'Shock and disbelief in the main, but also confusion. It's about the only thing that's being talked about—wild speculation and conjecture. I guess that's to be expected.'

'Agreed. Now I need to run, chat later.'

On seeing the lanky figure of D.S. Pillay on the court building steps, he pocketed his phone. 'Hey, Dhanraj, hold up a moment.'

Pillay turned and greeted him.

'I'm not sure I thanked you for allowing Jeremy to have a change of clothing and bedding and, of course, decent food. I'm grateful, as was he. We've been best friends most of our lives.'

'Think nothing of it,' said Pillay.

'This is a nasty business. I'm sure you'll get to the truth.'

'Why aren't you representing him as counsel?' asked Pillay. 'Right now, you're one of the top criminal lawyers around.'

'That's kind of you to say so, but it wouldn't be appropriate given our close friendship; instead I'll be helping out with the investigative work for the defence team, so we'll be seeing a lot of each other. Hopefully we can continue enjoying the professional relationship we've always had?'

'Of course. Each of us has a job to do and, as always, we'll do it properly and with mutual respect, I'm sure.'

'Can I ask you about your boss, Kumalo? What's he like? I've not dealt with him before.'

Pillay hesitated a tad too long before responding, rubbing his chin between thumb and index finger, and grimacing ever so slightly. 'He's new to the squad, so I don't know him all that well. Ex-Financial Intelligence Services. From what I've seen, he's one tough nut—seen it all, done it all—thorough and exceptionally clever, and when he has the bit between his teeth there's no stopping him. And he has a fiery temper.'

'But is he honest and fair?'

'I've no reason to think otherwise, but I must warn you he's terribly suspicious of lawyers, having been burnt a few times.'

'Mm, you mentioned that the other day. Thanks for the warning. I trust you'll allay his fears as far as I'm concerned,' said Gary, not expecting an answer. 'I'll send you a formal email shortly requesting copies of postmortem, pathology, DNA and forensic reports. I'd also like our experts to have access to all impounded evidence—you know, the usual, the deceased's clothing, Jeremy's clothing, any crime scene exhibits, Jeremy's car, etcetera.'

'Send it to Kumalo and cc me,' replied Pillay. 'He's rather fussy about wanting everything to go through him.'

'Will do. I gather from comments made by Kumalo during Jeremy's interview that there are no eyewitnesses at this stage?'

'There rarely are in these cases. It's all about circumstantial evidence and at the moment, I'm sorry to say, things aren't looking good for your friend. However, let's not prejudge.'

'You're right, Dhanraj, it's early days. For what it's worth, I've known him a long time and there is no way he raped or killed that girl. No way.'

Gary's phone vibrated as he stepped into the dentist's reception for his four o'clock appointment. 'Hey, Jeremy, anything urgent? I'm about to see the dentist. Can I call you back in half an hour?'

'It can wait. I wanted to let you know about a phone call a few minutes ago from David Plaistowe.'

'They're waiting for me. I'll swing by when I'm done here.'

'Perfect; see you then.'

During the drive to the Winters' family home Gary returned the call from the *Chronicle* journalist, ducking her probing questions about Amanda's death. 'If you want to pursue this, I suggest you get hold of David Plaistowe, the chairperson of the firm.'

'But why did you resign?' she asked. 'Were you pushed because of your close friendship with Jeremy Winters and the scandal of two years ago?'

'I don't think it's appropriate to discuss my resignation.'

'But why not?'

'I have nothing more to say, I'm sorry. Speak to David Plaistowe.'

The glistening black sports car wound its way up the long, paved driveway towards the house, snaking through the blossoming jacaranda trees on either side. Gary heard a familiar popping sound as his wheels crushed the mauve carpet of petals. In the distance Jeremy waved enthusiastically from the patio.

Out in the gazebo at the far end of the garden Jeremy told Gary about his suspension at work.

'I bet David showed no empathy or support,' said Gary, topping up his tall glass with cold beer.

'Stuff all. He made no bones about the firm and clients coming first. He said the firm couldn't be seen to be associating with me during this time, which is why you had resigned. Is that true, Gary?'

'It's true,' said Gary, giving Jeremy the correct context for his resignation.

'My dear friend, you didn't have to do that on my account. Now you're without work.'

'Hopefully I'll find something else quite quickly. In any event, I want to be free so I can focus on your case.'

'But you're crazy to give up your job. You won't find anything close to your position at Plaistowe's. I never expected you to do that.'

'You are my closest and dearest friend and my bonds with your family are there for life.' Gary didn't elaborate, knowing Jeremy understood.

Jeremy leaned forward and clinked glasses. 'I'm humbled, and don't know how I'll ever be able to repay you. This means so much to me, and to my folks.'

'Let's not forget what happened to Annie, and that's something that'll remain with me forever.'

Jeremy reached out, touching Gary's shoulder and closing his eyes for a moment before changing the subject. 'I don't relish the idea of garden leave, though. I wish I could be in touch with my clients to tell them I'm innocent.'

'You could resign and then tell them,' proffered Gary.

'The thought has crossed my mind but, sadly, I need my salary, and no one will take me on with this crap hanging over my head. Besides, can you imagine the reaction—the managing partners will want an undertaking from me not to contact clients and if I refuse, they'll go to court to stop me.'

'I don't think so, because inevitably that will bring the previous scandal back into the open. They wouldn't want to go there.'

'I hear you, but it's academic. I need the money.'

Jeremy's parents joined them briefly, bringing some more cold beer. They all held up their glasses. Jeremy's dad said, 'Here's to the two of you; strength to you, son, and thanks to you, Gary. We'll beat this thing, whatever it takes.'

After they left, Gary and Jeremy talked about the way forward and the challenges lying ahead.

'Our difficulty,' said Gary, 'is that you can't remember what happened after you and Amanda left the party, so you can't explain the state in which the police found you, relatively close to Amanda's body. On top of this, my guess is that DNA analysis will show the panties found in your jacket pocket belonged to her.'

'But,' interjected Jeremy, 'that doesn't prove I harmed her, surely? We may have got it on in the car.'

'I agree. The police are going to make a meal of your denials at the first interview. They'll also ask why, if you guys had consensual intimacy, Amanda strayed from the car into the stairwell.'

'Maybe because she wanted to go home and lost her way.'

'They'll also argue there is no evidence that anyone else was in the area and therefore it could only have been you.'

'How can they say that? Is the area monitored by cameras or by anyone?'

'This is one of many points to be followed up. I know there are CCTV cameras in the Baobab Ballroom and in the lobby area outside. I'm planning to get in touch with the hotel to ask for access. We need to stay positive and take one step at a time. These types of investigations are generally long and drawn out.'

'How long?'

'Varies,' said Gary. 'Could take weeks or even months where DNA analysis is involved. The labs have huge backlogs.'

'Months? You've got to be kidding,' said Jeremy. 'I'm not sure I've got the stamina.'

Gary took hold of Jeremy's upper arms, and faced him. 'Listen to me, I know what I'm talking about. Be prepared for the long haul. You must take on something to keep yourself busy otherwise you'll go crazy—maybe a course of some kind.'

'Do you really think so?' asked Jeremy.

'Yes, definitely. I've seen this movie many times and I know what lies ahead. If you have nothing to keep yourself occupied, you'll end up brooding the hours away, and that's not good.'

'I hear you. I'll see what I can come up with. Maybe the time's come for me to become that scratch golfer I've always wanted to be.'

'That's the spirit. By the way,' said Gary, 'I've already sent a formal request to the police for copies of their forensic reports, and for access to all clothing and crime scene exhibits. Our experts will examine everything closely. If nothing else, we must punch holes in their circumstantial evidence.'

'I want more than that,' said Jeremy. 'I need more. We must prove who raped and killed Amanda, otherwise, even if I'm not charged, some people will be suspicious for the rest of my life. You can imagine what that'll do, not only to my career but also to my life generally.'

'You're right. Any plans for Friday? The psychiatrist Professor East can slot you in for an initial consultation. He's eminently qualified to give an opinion on blackouts.'

'That's fine.'

'Okay. I'll firm up the appointment and keep in touch.'

On his way out, Gary popped into the kitchen to say goodbye to Mr and Mrs Winters. 'Thank you for the drinks and please feel free to contact me at any time, and I mean any time, if there is anything you need or want to know.'

Jeremy followed him out to the car. Gary folded his huge frame into the compact sports car. 'We'll find the person who did this, Jeremy, that's my promise to you.'

5

Waiting his turn at the Egoli Hotel reception, Gary made a hurried call. It had been seven days since Amanda's death in which he had attended her funeral, appointed a legal team to defend Jeremy, and had begun his own investigations into the events of that terrible night.

'Hello, Lucy, sorry I haven't been in touch. It's been hellishly hectic. I can't believe we're already a week on.'

'No problem, I know you're tied up. How're things?'

'Jeremy's holding up even though the stress is debilitating at times. His time with Professor East went as expected. He sees him again in the next few days. I might have to cut this call, I'm at the Egoli for a meeting. Could you find out what taxi arrangements the firm made for staff after the party? Sorry, got to run —will call later.'

He stepped towards the receptionist, informing her of his appointment with the general manager. 'Take a seat, Mr Edwards, I'll let Mr Strachan know you're here.'

After a few minutes he was in the glass elevator that hugged the outside of the building, being whisked to the twenty-first floor. No sooner had he begun taking in the magnificent view when the faceless voice announced the end of the ride. As the doors opened a dapper middle-aged gentleman introduced himself as Gunter Strachan. 'Follow me please,' he said politely, leading the way to his office where they made themselves comfortable in leather armchairs adjacent to a large window.

'Thank you, Mr Strachan, for making time. As I mentioned over the phone, I was one of the Plaistowe partners who attended the firm's party here at your hotel and I'm helping the defence team find out what exactly happened. There are many who are impacted by the events of that night, many at the firm as well as family and friends of the victim, and others.'

'Please call me Gunter. What a terrible shock. In my thirty plus years I've never had anything like this happen. I'm deeply sorry.'

'Like you, Gunter, we too are shocked. Our concern right now is to gather any information that might clarify how this tragedy came about. I'm liaising with Detective Sergeant Pillay of the Murder and Robbery Squad. He and I go back many years.'

'I met Sergeant Pillay a few days ago when he and Captain Kumalo paid a visit. He told me someone had been arrested.'

'Only as a suspect. I happen to know him, and I can assure you he's not capable of this.'

'Well, we're here to help in whatever way we can. Now, what can I do for you?'

'If I'm going to call you Gunter please call me Gary. We appreciate your willingness to help. It would be helpful to know how your access controls work, particularly as regards time-in, time-out, car and driver identity, etcetera.'

'We're a luxury establishment with an international reputation and the hotel strictly adheres to best practices as the safety of our guests and their belongings is of paramount importance.'

He explained that the image of each car and driver is captured by CCTV cameras, both at the time of entering and exiting the hotel parkade, with the date and precise time of entry and exit being automatically recorded. Furthermore, the security guards at the points of entry and exit maintain a register which each driver must complete and sign.

'The register calls for the driver's name, the number of passengers, the purpose of the visit, the name of the driver's company or firm, if any, the driver's phone number and the time of entry or exit. In addition to all of this,' said Gunter, 'the identity document, passport or driver's licence of each driver is scanned, both at the time of entry and exit.'

'Impressive,' said Gary. 'Multiple layers of control.'

'Some think too many, but I'm pleased we have them,' replied Gunter, sitting a little taller and rubbing his hands together.

'What about CCTV cameras in the basement parking areas and the stairwells between them?' asked Gary.

'There aren't any. We've considered the need a few times, but in the end decided against it.'

'And in the Baobab Ballroom and its points of entry and exit?'

'All covered. Let's go down and I'll show you,' invited Gunter.

The short conducted tour convinced Gary that any movement in and out of the ballroom and outside the lobby elevators servicing the basements would be recorded. 'Does the CCTV footage automatically record the time?'

'Yes. Our system is top of the range digital video recording which also allows for easy review.'

'I see there's a closed door to the far left of the elevators. Where does that lead and is it covered by a camera?'

'It leads to a stairwell that goes all the way down to the lowest parking basement. Regrettably the camera for that door was faulty and out of operation over the weekend of your party. I did let your firm know.'

'Is there any way to access the parking basements other than via these stairs or elevators?'

'The only other way is through the car entrance.'

'What access points into and out of the hotel are there besides the parkade and front door points?'

'The staff and tradespeople have one access point, but they can't get down to the parking basements except through the parkade entrance or by using the elevators or stairwell.'

'Okay, understood, thank you. When would it be convenient to look at the registers and CCTV footage?' asked Gary, being careful not to let on that his investigation was a private one.

'I can help you on the CCTV footage, but I'm afraid the police took away the registers.'

'Don't you have copies?'

'We didn't have time to make any. Here's the business card of our head of security systems and operations. If you don't mind, liaise directly with him. He'll probably need a day's warning to set things up for the CCTV footage.'

'Great, I'll do that. If you need to get hold of me give me a shout on my mobile. I need to be as discreet as possible for reasons I'm sure you'll understand.'

Gunter frowned without giving a response.

On exiting the hotel, Gary called Lucy again. 'Hey, that took a while—excellent meeting with the G.M. He's agreed for me to look at the CCTV footage but unfortunately the police have already taken away the car access registers. As I said earlier, I'm keen to find out whether firm personnel had the usual taxi facility after the party and, if so, whether there is a record anywhere of the folks who used it, the times of use and the addresses where they were dropped off.'

'That arrangement was in place because I for one used it. The driver recorded my name. I've no idea whether he made a record of the time and my home address. I can check that. We had to book a slot through the firm and provide details of our drop-off address.'

'Any chance of laying your hands on a copy of the booking sheet?'

'Not sure. I'll try. I'm intrigued, what are you after?'

'I think a useful starting point is to focus on people movements in and out of the party and the hotel, in the hope of picking up some clues. Lucy, be careful. David Plaistowe can be brutal if you cross him, so you need to be discreet.'

'I'll do my best, but if David finds out, then so be it; that's a risk I'm willing to take. Anyway, I'm glad you called. Since the funeral there's been a heaviness in the air at the office, a deep sadness, and, at the same time, anger about the loss of a young life in such a cruel way. Some people are becoming more and more resentful, hoping Jeremy will, quote, rot in hell, unquote. It's quite ugly, and Roger stokes the flames whenever he can. I can't understand why he's being so vindictive.'

'I guess these different reactions aren't unexpected,' said Gary. 'It's as well that Jeremy didn't attend. I can't remember when last I saw so many people at a funeral —I suspect some were curious onlookers or members of the press. It was great to see a good attendance from the firm, including all the managing partners. I have to say, I came away with mixed emotions about the purpose of life and wondering where God was in all this.'

'I know what you mean, Gary. I always find funerals unsettling that leave me with bad dreams for days after. Amanda and I were of a similar age. That could've been me, or any young woman for that matter. I can't even begin to imagine how a decent human like Jeremy could possibly do this, and that's why I refuse to believe he was the one.'

'As for Roger, I can understand him being jealous of Jeremy,' said Gary, 'and perhaps showing this in various ways. But to stoke the flames, as you put it, is beyond me. Why the hell would he do that?'

'He's always acted the big deal in the office, but this time he's going too far. And by the way, he's telling anyone who cares to listen how he's going to sue you and have you prosecuted for assault. He loves to flaunt his *royalty* as the chairperson's son. Silly jerk.'

'Thanks, Lucy. Let's see if he follows through.'

Later that day he called Pillay. 'Gary Edwards here, a quick one. I understand you guys have taken some registers from the Egoli Hotel. Please could you make copies for me?'

'I don't see a problem, but first pop Captain Kumalo an email with a cc to me, making your request.'

'Will do. Any developments since we last chatted?'

'Nothing of consequence. On your side?'

'Much the same; it's still early days. The press are having a field day, dragging his name through the mud.'

'When do you expect the postmortem report and the DNA results?'

'The P.M. should be to hand any day now, but the DNA results could take some weeks. We're pushing the lab.'

'I haven't heard back from Kumalo on the list of crime scene items. Besides the obvious ones, such as Jeremy's car and clothing and the deceased's clothing and clutch bag, and the pair of black panties, what else was there?'

'I'm sure he'll get back to you. He's been under pressure. There's one item you're probably not aware of: an empty champagne bottle found next to the deceased's body. It appeared to have some light blood smears. These are being tested. But keep that to yourself. If Kumalo knows I'm passing on information he'll skin me alive.'

'Thanks, you can trust me. One more small point, if I may? Were there any signs the deceased had been assaulted with the bottle?'

'Gary, you're taking advantage now, please. Last favour—it appeared she had been hit on the forehead. That's it, no more.'

Mr Winters ran towards Gary's car as it pulled up to the family home. He shuffled from one foot to the other and intermittently rubbed his hands together as he waited impatiently for Gary to get out of the car. Frowning, and with a downward curve of the top lip, Mr Winters thanked him for coming at such short notice. 'I'm terribly worried, Jeremy's not coping; he's not sleeping well with all the nightmares, and eating next to nothing.'

Reaching out, Gary placed a hand on Mr Winters' upper arm. 'So sorry to hear that, but not altogether surprised. He must be going through hell right now. When's he due to see Professor East again?'

'In the next couple of days. Come, let's go in and you can see for yourself.'

Jeremy and his mother joined them in the sunroom. His hair hadn't seen a brush for days and his face appeared drawn, with dark rings under his sunken eyes. Stepping back from their hug, Gary looked down into the dull eyes. 'I know it's tough, my friend, but this is only the beginning. You must tell the prof about how you're feeling, your nightmares and loss of appetite.'

'I will,' said Jeremy in a soft, shaky voice. 'It's awful. I have this constant gnawing fear like a sense of foreboding, and I feel flat and not interested in anything. I'm beginning to wonder whether I did do something stupid and merely wiped it from my memory. I'm confused.'

Gary steered him to a couch. 'What you're going through isn't unusual. I've seen it before. Look at me, pal,' he said, grabbing Jeremy by the shoulders. 'It's vital you tell all this to Professor East. It will be relevant to his assessment, and he needs to give you something to manage the stress. Have you taken on anything to keep yourself busy?'

'No, I can't find it in me. I feel mentally and emotionally paralysed.'

Mrs Winters slid in on the other side of her son, stretching out a motherly arm over his shoulders. He pulled the bottom of his shirt up to his face and wiped at his eyes. 'There's something else. I don't think it's anything to worry about—I'm not sure which way to go.'

'Go on,' encouraged Gary, not knowing what to expect.

'My memory seems to be coming back, but only in dribs and drabs. Some bits are clear and some quite foggy and some are simply missing. Should I be telling Professor East about this?'

'Yes, why not?' asked Gary with a frown.

'Here's the thing. As you know, I didn't tell the police I had a blackout, and they will no doubt make a meal of that.'

'Listen, and listen carefully, there's only one right way here and that's to tell it as you know it—no guessing, no manipulating, no adjusting your story in anticipation of what Kumalo and his team may do or come up with. It's simple—tell the truth. East will probably say this isn't unusual. I mean, it's happening to you, so it can't be impossible. What have you remembered?'

Before Jeremy could answer, Mr Winters got up and took his wife's hand. 'Come, dear, I think we should leave so they can get on discussing whatever needs to be discussed.' Mr Winters replenished their empty cups and passed over the plate of eats before departing.

'I have flashes of Amanda and me dancing... how do I say this... you know, intimately, and even kissing occasionally. I seem to recall us feeling horny, wanting to find somewhere private. Both of us were drunk. My next recollection is of us having sex in my car. I can't remember the finer detail. I don't know how my shirt came off or how her panties—I assume they were hers —came to be in my jacket pocket. How it ended or how or why she left, I don't remember.'

'Any recollection on taking a bottle of champagne with you?'

'I've racked my brain but can't remember. Why do you ask?'

'Pillay told me earlier today the police recovered a champagne bottle with light blood smears next to Amanda's body. They believe she had been struck on the head.'

'That's a bit of good news, isn't it, Gary? The person who hit Amanda would've left fingerprints on the bottle. Not so?'

'Could be, unless he wiped the bottle. I guess we'll know soon enough.'

'I hope there are prints because they won't be mine.'

'Don't get too excited; there's every chance some of your prints will be on there.'

'Well then, there should be two sets of prints: mine and those of the thug that did this.'

6

'Hello, Captain Kumalo, Gary Edwards here.'

'Yes,' came the terse reply.

Clutching the phone to his ear, Gary drifted over to the study window overlooking his manicured garden and watched Charlie splayed out in the shallow water lapping over the top step of the pool.

'Are you there, Mr Edwards?'

'Apologies, Captain, for a moment I was distracted by Charlie.'

'Who is Charlie? I don't know what the hell you're talking about.'

'He's the most incredible staffie on this planet and very special to me.'

'You called,' snapped Kumalo, showing no interest in Charlie.

'I'm following up to check whether any of the requested reports or items are yet available. I'm concerned that the Christmas holidays are on top of us, and people will soon be scooting off.'

'You of all people should know the labs can't be rushed. Their backlog is massive,' came the abrupt response.

'Of course, I understand, but surely the postmortem report and copies of the parking registers are available by now, and presumably there's no risk to your investigation if our experts are given access to Mr Winters' car?'

A long silence followed before Kumalo responded. 'I must've misunderstood your emails. I thought you wanted reports and access all at the same time and not piecemeal.'

Gary held the phone at arm's length. 'You smart arse, you know that's BS,' he murmured.

'What's that, Mr Edwards? I can't hear you.'

'Nothing—I was mumbling something to Charlie.'

'I'll email the postmortem report to you now and your experts can have access to the car anytime. Contact Pillay. You can also collect copies of the registers from him.'

'Thank you, Captain Kumalo, appreciated. Anything significant from the P.M. report, the car or the registers?'

Another long silence followed. 'I'm not in the habit of sharing information about an investigation until and unless I'm required to do so by law. So, no comment.'

'Okay, Captain, I'm beginning to get your drift. Perhaps you need to know where I'm coming from. I will insist on full and expeditious disclosure of all investigation information in line with Mr Winters' constitutional rights. I much prefer to cooperate with the police on these things provided the cooperation cuts both ways. I was hoping you and I could enjoy a courteous and reasonable relationship, but that seems not to be the case. I await the P.M. report and will contact Pillay shortly. And please send me the list I requested, it's long overdue.'

Kumalo didn't bother commenting.

Within minutes the postmortem report, together with the list of impounded crime scene items, arrived in Gary's inbox. He held his breath as he opened the attachments and sighed with relief on seeing the name of the attending pathologist. Dr Burnett enjoyed considerable respect amongst her peers and colleagues, whilst judicial officers and lawyers alike held her in high esteem.

He began to read. In Burnett's opinion, Amanda had been raped and then strangled to death. Her report confirmed the trauma to her head, noting the injury to be consistent with a moderate blow from a blunt object, such as a champagne bottle. She concluded that the blow would almost certainly have stunned Amanda and probably rendered her unconscious for a short period. The report described the bruising on Amanda's throat and the fracture of the hyoid bone, caused by strangulation. Bruising was also evident on both wrists, legs, back and buttocks. In the pathologist's opinion these bruises were strongly indicative of the victim, a small woman of slender build, having been held down with force. The vaginal swabs and fingernail scrapings had been referred for DNA analysis.

No surprises lurked in the list of crime scene items except for the fact that the contents of Amanda's clutch bag didn't include any keys, alarm remote control or cellphone.

Two days later, on a quiet Saturday morning, Gary collected Lucy and Jeremy in his other car, a Pajero 4x4, and drove to the Egoli Hotel to meet the head of hotel security, Rubin, and Chris Plumtree, a CCTV expert. Lucy sat in the front passenger seat while Jeremy cut a forlorn figure sitting alone in the back. On the way, Gary asked about his meeting with Professor East.

'It went well,' he said with a lightness in his voice not heard since his arrest. 'He thinks my patchy amnesia is not unusual, given the heavy drinking on top of my meds, and he said that recollection of recent events can return in different ways. It can be slow and fragmented, and I may never recall the blocked-out events entirely. He wants to see me again before drawing final conclusions.'

'What about your nightmares and loss of appetite?' enquired Gary.

'You were right, he thinks that's normal in my situation. He prescribed some meds and gave me a lecture about the dangers of mixing booze and painkillers.'

Lucy stretched back, and lightly touched Jeremy's arm. For a prolonged moment she stared at his handsomeness, accentuated by his icy blue eyes.

'That's exactly what we've been hoping for,' said Gary. 'It ties in with what you've been saying all along. The police will of course insist you're lying about your amnesia.'

'But how can they?' came a plaintiff cry from the back. 'Surely Professor East's opinion will be conclusive?'

'Not so,' said Gary. 'All he can say is that your version of the amnesia is not inconsistent with medical science. He can't say whether or not you are in fact suffering from amnesia.'

'How then do we prove Jeremy's version is true?' asked Lucy.

'You'll have to give evidence, Jeremy, and come across as truthful.'

After a brief lull in their conversation, Gary brought up the postmortem report. 'Lucy, please pass that yellow folder to Jeremy. A copy for you to read at your leisure,' said Gary, summarising the pertinent points. 'We're here, so let's chat more about this later.'

Rubin and Chris were waiting for them in reception.

'Thank you both for making time on a Saturday morning,' said Gary, 'most appreciated, particularly as Lucy can only get away from work outside office hours. Chris, I understand Rubin has shown you the setup, so when you're ready, let's get going.'

'I'll leave you guys to it,' said Rubin. 'I'll be in the office next door if you need anything.'

They started viewing from the Saturday 9 p.m. marker, fast forwarding the footage periodically. As expected, by ten o'clock the party was in full swing: subdued lighting, packed dance floor, some folks sitting at the tables, others standing in small groups, drinking, and chatting, and a few on their own, watching the festivity.

'Look there,' said Gary, pointing out Jeremy and Amanda on the dance floor obviously having fun and enjoying each other's company.

Jeremy remained quiet, absorbed in the unfolding scene. Lucy moved closer and whispered, 'You'll get through this.'

By the 11 p.m. marker the tempo had ratcheted up a few notches. Many of the senior partners still hung around. A few of them surrendered to the festive atmosphere, drinking heavily and at times even flirting with the staff. David Plaistowe, a teetotaler, swanned around, stopping periodically to chat, shake a hand or pat a shoulder.

Other members of staff entered the frame.

'Urgh, look at him,' groaned Lucy. 'I can't stand that man.'

'Who?' asked Gary.

'Surely you know. That creep Bagley-Smith. He's always perving at the young women in the office and making inappropriate comments. He's been caught a few times trying to look up skirts. Some of the girls in the tax practice are wary of him, particularly when he offers to give them a lift home after working late.'

'So I hear,' said Gary.

Their attention returned to the image of Jeremy and Amanda who by that point seemed oblivious to the fact that they were in a public place, surrounded by hundreds of onlookers. Close to the 11.30 p.m. marker they shuffled off, slowly meandering through the crowd towards the lobby, holding onto each other. Jeremy clutched a bottle of champagne in his free hand.

Chris switched footage, bringing the lobby elevators up on the screen. The amorous couple stumbled into the first available elevator, latching on to each other, and kissing passionately before the doors drew shut. They appeared to be unaware of two people in the corner, and clueless about Amanda's short black dress having crept up, revealing sheer black underwear.

'Chris, zoom in on the elevator's floor indicator, I want to see at which level they stop,' said Gary.

The elevator descended rapidly stopping only once, at the fifth parking basement, before returning empty to the lobby area. Gary, noticing Jeremy's agitation, took hold of his friend's left elbow and steered him quietly out of the room and down the corridor.

'Wait here, pal, I'm going to grab some refreshments from next door.' He returned with cool drinks and snacks in hand and found a quiet spot in an empty office close by.

Jeremy drained his drink and nibbled at a snack. Colour returned to his face and his breathing settled into an even rhythm.

'I know this is awkward and painful for you,' said Gary, 'but we've got to keep going until we find what we're looking for. Somewhere out there are the clues. If we search thoroughly, we'll find them. You needn't watch if this is too much for you.'

'That doesn't look good for me', said Jeremy, hands on hips and shaking his head. 'We're all over each other, making my denials to the police look like lies. And the black panties were obviously hers—something I told the police I had no knowledge of. Then there's the champagne bottle in my hand. This is terrible. I've had it.'

Gary stepped closer. 'I know this is difficult and that things appear hopeless. We've been over this before. So, you and Amanda were drunk and the two of you probably drank more champagne and had sex in your car, but that's a far cry from proving you raped and killed her. *Vasbyt*, be courageous, and we'll get through this.'

Jeremy elected to continue with the viewing. He composed himself, and they made their way back to the screening room.

'Did anyone recognise the other people in the elevator?' asked Gary.

Jeremy didn't, but Lucy did. 'That's Jilly Zandberg and Zara Wolensky from the accounts department. I know them quite well.'

She shuffled closer to Jeremy as reviewing resumed. Other elevators descended periodically but none beyond the third parking basement. As the marker showed 12.40 a.m., Roger Plaistowe, the chairperson's son, staggered into an elevator, almost bowling over the two couples ahead of him. The elevator stopped at the third parking basement before returning empty to the lobby.

The screening room descended into silence with all eyes fixed on the flickering screen. As the night of the party drew on they anticipated increased traffic in the lobby. Fourteen minutes later a small group gathered outside the elevators. All of them, except a lone, partially obscured woman, stepped into one elevator. She chose an empty elevator.

The elevator with the small group offloaded passengers at basements one, two and four. The other stopped at five.

'Did you guys see that?' asked Lucy. 'The lone woman got off at the fifth parking basement.'

'I also saw that', said Gary. 'Back up, Chris, I want a better view of her face.' After three reruns Gary and Lucy looked at each other and shrugged shoulders.

'It's hard to tell. We see so little of her', said Lucy. 'The bit I saw of her dress and shoes didn't help. So similar to many others.'

The elevators soon became busier, and at times were congested with revellers heading home.

'Hey, that's unusual,' exclaimed Chris suddenly. 'Someone's returning to the lobby.'

Everyone huddled closer, scrutinising the screen while Chris backed up. There, exiting the elevator at 1.20 a.m. before staggering out of sight, was the unmistakable drunken figure of Roger Plaistowe.

'Why would he be coming back?' asked Lucy.

'He may have left something at the party, or he might have gone to his car to fetch something,' said Gary. 'He could, I suppose, have changed his mind about leaving and decided to party some more. Roll on, Chris, let's see what else there is.'

A few more revellers entered the elevators, but only one of them headed down to the fifth parking basement. 'There's your favourite, Lucy,' said Gary, 'getting off at the fifth—Sebastian "Pervert" Bagley-Smith.'

'I'm surprised he isn't in an elevator full of young women,' snorted Lucy.

At 1.55 a.m., about thirty-five minutes after Roger's return, he and his father arrived in the lobby in animated conversation, and summoned an elevator.

'That's why he came back,' said Jeremy, sounding deflated. 'He came to call daddy, probably to be driven home.'

The elevator stopped at the fifth parking basement where it remained.

Except for a few stragglers who wandered into the lobby over the next half hour, there were no more movements in the area. The party was all but over.

'Something's bothering me,' commented Gary. 'Can we do a rerun from the time Jeremy and Amanda leave the party. My notes show 11.30 p.m. I want to check the basement level to which Roger went.'

Lucy spoke first after the rerun. 'That's strange. The first time he got off at the third basement and yet he and his father head to the fifth. If Roger's car was parked on the third, why would he now be going to the fifth?'

'That is odd', replied Jeremy. 'And if he had parked on the fifth why did he get off on the third? And why did he catch the elevator on the third when returning?'

'And there's no chance the old man parked in either the third or the fifth basement; he would have had reserved parking at ground level,' noted Gary. 'Let's put a pin in that for the time being. There are a couple of other things I want to check before we call it a day. Roll back to about nine o'clock. I'm keen to see who took an elevator down to the basements before Jeremy and Amanda headed down.'

Except for a few couples and some women on their own, no one of interest used the elevators immediately before Jeremy and Amanda's departure.

'Now, let's check the time Bagley-Smith left,' said Gary.

'There,' said Chris, stopping the image at 1.25 a.m. 'He gets off at the fifth.'

'I wouldn't have thought as a managing partner he would've parked so far down,' remarked Lucy.

'Does seem a bit funny,' said Gary. 'Will also put a pin in that one. We've been at it for hours and I'm sure, like me, you must be exhausted. We'll have to pick up on the parking entrance footage at some other time. Lucy, any chance you could have a chat to the accounts department couple to check if they saw or heard anything unusual before they parted company with Jeremy and Amanda?'

'Sure, will let you know.'

7

The incessant buzzing intruded on Gary's sleep. He stared vacantly into the darkness, uncertain about the irritating noise. The luminous bedside clock showed 1.27 a.m. After a few moments he registered the source of the noise and searched for his phone on the nearside table. It wasn't there. Finally, the buzzing ceased, allowing him to roll onto his back, grateful that he could reunite with his sleep. Suddenly the noise intruded again from the other side of the bed. He leaned across with a grunt, searching amongst the sheets before latching onto his mobile phone.

'Hello, Mr Winters, what's the problem?'

'Sorry to call at this time,' stammered Mr Winters in a panicky voice, 'but we need your urgent help—it's Jeremy.'

Gary quickly pulled on a track suit. 'Is he hurt?'

'No, but emotionally out of control, teetering on the edge.'

'Should I call an ambulance?'

'Not yet, if you're able to get here soon.'

'Okay, keep a close eye on him. I'm leaving now.'

Mrs Winters, dressed in her nightgown and *sans* makeup, met him at the front door. The tissue in her hand had been wrung into a tiny ball and her cheeks and nose were wet and red.

'Tell me quickly, what happened?' said Gary.

'About half an hour before calling you we heard a bloodcurdling scream. It was terrifying.' She wiped at her nose and struggled to get the words out. 'I've never heard anything like it. It was Jeremy.' She paused, again wiping her nose with the remnants of the tissue.

'Steady on, Mrs Winters. I'll take care of it. Tell me the rest.'

'We rushed to his room and found him curled up on the floor with a sheet pulled over his head. He kept shouting, "I did it, I did it, I killed her." He was shaking and crying at the same time and hasn't stopped since then. These nightmares are haunting our child. We don't know what to do.'

Gary followed her to the dimly lit room where they found Jeremy back on his bed. His father, in close attendance, gave Gary a hastened wave. It was sad and worrying to see his friend in such a state. Gary sat on the edge of the bed, rubbing the palm of his hand slowly across the back of the sobbing figure in the foetal position, shaking uncontrollably.

'Hey, Jeremy, it's me.'

The sobbing became louder and the shaking more pronounced.

Trying again, he asked, 'What's up, pal, what's happening?'

Still no reply.

'I'm here to help. What can I do?' asked Gary looking at the forlorn figure, then at his parents and back at his friend.

After waiting patiently, but still rubbing Jeremy's back, he heard muffled murmurings between the sobs. Gary moved to the opposite side of the bed so he could make eye contact. 'What was that, my friend?'

Although the crying and shaking abated slightly, Jeremy remained curled up. Gary squeezed his upper arm and leaned forward to hear better.

'I'm losing it,' came a broken whisper. 'I don't know how much more I can take.' He fell silent; Gary gently prodded him. 'Talk to me, Jeremy, I'm worried and want to help.'

'Every night I have these recurring nightmares of me raping and strangling Amanda. They are so real, and every morning I wake up and remember I've got this tag around my ankle... it makes me feel a criminal. I'm beginning to think I must have done it.' The sobbing and shaking returned as he coiled into a tighter ball.

Gary moved even closer. 'Listen to me, Jeremy. We've been best mates for more than twenty-five years and I'll never lie to you about this. I've no doubt that someone else did this and that we'll get to the truth. I'm no doctor, but you're under unbelievable stress and that can do strange things to your mind.'

Another prolonged silence. Gary waited patiently for his friend to come around.

'I'm so confused. I've lost control and feel like I'm having a breakdown. My life is ruined.'

'I think you must get an urgent appointment with Professor East later this morning and tell him what's happening. My guess is he'll adjust your medication. But you need to get some sleep. Mrs Winters, do you have any sleeping pills?'

'Is that a good idea, considering his other meds?'

'In the circumstances, it's probably the least worst option.'

She assented. 'Jeremy has some from his last visit to Prof East.'

She left the room and returned quickly with a tablet.

Jeremy sat up. His puffy red eyes accentuated the dark rings.

'Do you think I'm going mad, Gary? At times I don't know whether I'm hallucinating or recalling some forgotten detail of that night.'

'No, you're not going mad. Take this pill and get some sleep. I'll sit with you. And be sure to tell Professor East everything.'

By the time he left the Winters' home the glow of the rising sun had begun to paint the eastern skyline a soft golden colour. But what would the day bring for his friend?

Fifteen minutes late for his lunch at Lucy's favourite restaurant, Gary arrived somewhat frazzled. 'So sorry, but it's been a night and morning from hell. Couldn't call because I've misplaced my mobile. Can you believe it.'

'Not a problem, started without you,' she said, lifting a glass of chardonnay in a mock toast. 'What's going on?'

He told her about the early call. 'It was terribly sad to see him so broken. He was incoherent for much of the time. Apparently another nightmare triggered the episode.'

'That's worrying.'

'It is. His poor parents were visibly shaken. They didn't know what to do and feared he might harm himself. Anyway, after an hour or so I managed to calm him down. The sleeping pill soon knocked him out, but I hung around for a while, mostly to allow his folks to get some sleep. Thank goodness they managed to get an early appointment with Professor East. May I use your phone to give them a quick call?'

He briefly stepped outside. When he returned to the table he grabbed the glass of wine she had ordered for him and drained most of it before sitting down. 'The professor's strengthened his meds, with a caution, though, that his condition could suddenly deteriorate to the point of needing hospitalisation.'

Gary paused, staring out of the restaurant window, seemingly at nothing, and then continued. 'I'll visit him every day and, if need be, I'll sleep over. This is so unlike him. He's normally such a tough guy mentally. Over the years I've seen him in many stressful situations, and he's always coped well. You know, at work, many of the senior lawyers see him as the man for the task when things get tough.'

She caught his eye briefly before saying, 'You're a good mate, Gary Edwards. I wish there were more people like you in this world.'

He acknowledged the compliment and took a sip of his drink.

'What's happened to your mobile?' asked Lucy.

'I've no idea and can't think straight right now. I noticed it missing when I got to Pillay's office. And you won't believe it—Kumalo had hauled him off somewhere knowing that I had an appointment to collect the registers. They kept me waiting for over an hour. And to crown it all, on my way here I had a flat tyre. I'm terribly sorry, this was meant to be a relaxed thank you treat. How many years now? Six or seven?'

'Hey, not an issue, these things happen. I've been with you six years; a great six years I might add.'

'How time flies. You're the best,' he said lifting his glass in a toast. 'Do you have any regrets about not going into the business world after varsity?'

She smiled coyly. 'Not at all. I do hope that down the road I'll be able to get involved in law firm management.'

'That might happen sooner than you think,' he said.

Their conversation turned to his future and whether he might return to Plaistowe's when this ordeal was over. He told her he was sickened by the lack of any support from the firm for Jeremy and worried by the dramatic change in culture over the last few years, driven by David Plaistowe and his acolytes.

'I definitely won't be going back. It's become a toxic environment with far too much emphasis on money and power. Standards have dropped because the focus is wrong, and corners are being cut. It's only a matter of time before things begin to unravel.'

'That sounds too awful.'

'It is. I've been waiting for the right opportunity to come along so I could get out of there without taking a step backwards, but with this latest nonsense my mind is made up. I'll either hang out my own shingle or look for something at one of the boutique firms and bring you across if you're still keen.'

'Of course, I'm still keen,' she replied, handing him an envelope. 'And to prove how efficient I can be, here's something for you to look at later.'

'What's this?'

She explained they were copies of the taxi lists. One showed the names of all firm personnel who booked slots, as well as their drop-off addresses. 'The other list is a duplicate of the first,' she said, 'but also shows whether or not the service was used, and if so, who the taxi driver was, and the time and address at which the drop was made.'

'How did you manage to lay your hands on these?'

'Not too difficult in the end. My buddy in H.R. helped.'

'Thanks, Lucy, you're a champ. What are you eating or are you happy to trust me to order?'

She chose a sashimi and sushi platter and waited for him to place the order before she returned to business.

'It's important to compare the two documents,' she said. 'You'll see from the first list that Amanda booked an eleven forty-five slot to take her home to Rivonia. I was there on the day of the party after we shopped for our outfits. The second list confirms the obvious: she didn't use the taxi service.'

'Any luck on the couple from accounts?'

'I did manage a chat with them.'

'And?' prompted Gary impatiently.

'They've already been interviewed by the police and have been told not to speak to anyone else.'

'That's a pity; I wonder what they've said. I guess we'll find out when we see the police docket. And the lone woman?'

'No success there yet, so little to go on.'

'Maybe during tomorrow's CCTV footage review we'll pick up something. I'm keen to know if she saw or heard anything unusual.'

'If she did, surely by now she would've come forward.'

'Not necessarily,' said Gary, as their food arrived, 'she may be frightened or simply reluctant to get involved. Or perhaps she's also made a statement to the police.'

He turned his attention to the plate before him. 'Another glass of chardonnay?' he asked laughingly as a piece of sashimi slipped from his chopsticks, splashing soy sauce over the front of his light blue shirt.

She leaned across and dabbed at the damage. 'Tut-tut, you messy boy. Thank you, I will have another, seeing it's my afternoon off.'

Gary called the order to an idle waitress. Lucy then asked for his honest opinion on Jeremy's chances.

'There's no way he could have done this, surely? You saw them in the elevator. Of course, Amanda may have changed her mind, and if she did, Jeremy would've respected that, I've no doubt. But how does he explain his denials to the police? Isn't this where Professor East's evidence will help? He'll say, I hope, that Jeremy was suffering from amnesia at the interview.'

'I wish it were that simple,' said Gary. 'East won't be able to say Jeremy did in fact have amnesia. All he can say is blackouts from binge drinking, when combined with Jeremy's meds, are not unusual and that what Jeremy described to him, about his own position, is consistent with him suffering from a blackout. I think— I hope—he'll also say that a person suffering from a blackout could genuinely believe the blackout events didn't happen.'

'That's good, isn't it?'

'Only up to a point. Unless we find evidence pointing to someone else, I'm afraid Jeremy's at risk, and the outcome, as I've said before, will then depend on how well he stands up under cross examination. That's why we must get him strong. In his present state he's likely to crumble'

She gasped and brought her hands up to her mouth. A tear spilled onto her cheek and rolled slowly down to her chin. He took hold of her hands, squeezing them softly. 'It's early days,' he said. 'We need to see the forensic reports and examine all the facts. If someone else did this, evidence will be there. We need to find it.'

'Honestly, Gary, do you think someone else did this?'

He hesitated.

'Why are you hesitating? You make me worried.'

'I love Jeremy, and he's the best friend I've ever had, and it's hard to think he may have had something to do with this—things aren't looking good—but I'm pushing on, believing, and hoping we'll find the culprit. But we're in a strange situation when he admits that he *could* have been responsible for a crime for which I'm sure he's innocent.'

They both took a swig of wine and pondered Jeremy's dilemma.

'You've got strong feelings for him, don't you, Lucy?'

She paused before replying. 'We've been good friends for a long time, since I started working at Plaistowe's. I think he's one of the nicest human beings I know. To be open, yes, I've recently been developing feelings for him on a deeper level.'

'How did you feel about seeing him with Amanda?'

'A little jealous I guess, but I don't think they had any sort of serious relationship. Lots of booze, end of year, and victory celebrations—a sure cocktail for sexual fireworks.'

'He's a great guy. You should let him know how you feel. He likes you and has often talked about you.'

'Saying what, exactly?' she asked with an expectant look.

'That would be telling,' he teased.

'Oh, c'mon, please tell.'

'He thinks you have an engaging personality.'

'An *engaging personality*, really! My granny has an engaging personality.'

'Okay, he thinks you're gorgeous and sexy and that you're the kind of woman a man marries, quote unquote. There you have it. By the way, for what it's worth, I agree with him.'

She blushed, bringing her hands up to cover her small but beautifully proportioned angular face.

'That's so affirming, thank you', she said, changing the subject as she combed her fingers through her stylishly groomed bob. 'I know you guys have been friends a long time. Where did it all begin?'

'In our third year at school. After that we were in the same class for the rest of our schooling and played in the same sports teams. We were inseparable. And then, believe it or not, we ended up at the same university studying law before joining Plaistowe's.

We're closer than brothers and my bond with the Winter family is forever.'

'How come? You stand to lose so much and yet you're standing by Jeremy and being remarkably supportive of his folks.'

'Besides our long and sincere friendship, there's more, much more.'

She waited, but he seemed reticent about elaborating.

'You don't have to tell,' she said, shaking her head.

He reflected a while longer. 'I think you should know—I want you to know.'

He poured himself a glass of water and stared out of the window, chin resting on his clenched fists and elbows propped up on the table. Although he gave the appearance of someone struggling to recall past events, chilling details of that night remained in the forefront of his mind.

Before Lucy started to work for Gary, he dated Annie—Jeremy's younger sister. Their relationship became serious and they even talked about getting married someday, which would have made the two friends brothers-in-law. Gary felt a shiver down his spine as he began to share his painful memory with Lucy.

After visiting friends one evening in an unfamiliar part of the city, Gary took a shortcut to the Winters' home so that Annie could show off her new puppie to her parents. He could still hear Annie warning against the dangerous road.

His stomach churned as he relived the biggest regret of his life; he should have listened to Annie, but instead he told her not to be such a ninny. He recalled her tentative reply, word for word: 'I hope you know what you're doing, you have precious cargo on board.' She reached back, retrieved the puppy from his basket, and cuddled him. 'We'll be okay, Charlie, we'll be okay.'

Gary stretched out an arm and stroked Annie's neck. 'I love you very much, Annie Winters.'

He drove as fast as he could, mindful of the desolate road with its potholes and absence of street lights. The darkened road was devoid of traffic except for one other car a long way back. The emptiness of the neighbourhood forced him to wonder whether he had been foolish. For a few minutes he toyed with the idea of turning back but decided to push on when he saw traffic lights up ahead. Shortly after the intersection they would join up with a main road. Gary masked his apprehension about the road with small talk; Annie hugged Charlie close to her chest and kept her silence. Aware of her nervousness and irritation, he let her be.

He slowed as he approached the intersection and looked left and right to check if it was safe to jump the red light. A cursory glance at his rear-view mirror revealed the following vehicle had caught up and was now about thirty metres back. His eyes flicked back to the intersection as he readied himself to accelerate, but not before another vehicle crossed his path and stopped. His instincts screamed out 'danger' and the surge of adrenalin heightened all his senses. Hijack. For a moment, the imminent threat seemed to unfold in slow motion. A man wearing a balaclava jumped out of the stationary car at the intersection and brandished an AK-47 assault rifle in the air as he rapidly closed the distance between them.

Gary yelled at Annie to get down as he anxiously threw the gear stick into reverse and floored the accelerator, simultaneously pulling down hard right on the steering wheel. Tyres screeched as the car spun through 180 degrees, with the gunman now close behind them. Ahead, leaning against the other car, was a second gunman. Gary glimpsed a muzzle flash from the direction of the second gunman. Again Gary shouted at Annie to stay down as he jammed the gear stick into drive with his right foot still heavy on the accelerator.

Short bursts of automatic fire filled the air as his car shot forward, tyres spinning. The second gunman dived out of the way just in time to avoid being struck by Gary's car. More gunfire pierced the night air and then Gary heard glass shatter. The shooter was now on target. Annie's terrified voice cried out, 'I've got you, Charlie.'

Gary turned his face away from Lucy and rubbed his eyes. He took a drink and looked around the restaurant, but nobody noticed the trauma he was going through.

'You don't have to do this, Gary.'

'I want to tell you.'

Speeding away from the intersection, Gary's eyes flicked intermittently across his mirrors. The dazzling lights of the chasing vehicles became larger and brighter. There was little doubt they were closing in on him. It was then that he heard a most terrible noise, a gurgling sound, a sound he hoped never to hear. It was Annie. With each gurgle more blood pumped out of her mouth. He could smell it. Annie held on tightly to Charlie. Gary glanced up at the the mirror again—there was no way he could stop. The nearest hospital was less than five kilometres away. He leaned across and shook Annie by the shoulder; her body felt limp. He pleaded for her to answer him, but the only response was the gurgle. His chest thumped louder and faster. He withdrew his hand and felt the stickiness of her warm blood that was now covering her chest.

Despite the darkness and the state of the road, he sped as fast as his car would go. Their attackers continued to follow but seemed to drop back an appreciable distance, but not so far that he could stop and try to help Annie. At last the main road came into sight. Gary turned on his hazard warning lights. Seeing no car lights ahead on the main road, he reduced speed slightly to make his turn. The inside wheels left the road, tilting the car over at a dangerous angle. Gary battled with the steering wheel as the car skidded on two wheels before returning to upright, then fishtailed down the road as he fought to regain control.

Gary swerved in and out of traffic, hazards still flashing and his hand firmly on the horn. At last the attackers backed off and disappeared from sight. He could no longer hear any sound from Annie and prayed that she was still alive. The hospital lights came into view and he headed for the emergency and trauma gate, pulling up behind an ambulance. He jumped from the car and shouted. 'Please help! Someone please help! I have a shot passenger.' A medic came quickly, but it was too late.

Gary raised his eyes to Lucy. 'Annie's last words were, "I've got you, Charlie".'

He excused himself from the restaurant table. Lucy didn't follow.

After ten minutes he returned, patting Lucy on the shoulder before sitting down. 'Sorry about that—it's still painful. Eight years on and the guilt remains, even though the Winters have over and over said they don't blame me. That's why I'll always stand by them, no matter what.'

'I had no idea. I can't even begin to imagine the pain. I'm so sorry.'

'Not a good experience. At least I can hold on to the many wonderful memories I have of Annie, and Charlie is a constant reminder of the good times we had—she loved Charlie.'

Gary went quiet. She didn't interrupt his thoughts.

8

Christmas came and went quietly. Jeremy remained mostly stable and now, nearly two weeks later, Gary could at last continue reviewing the CCTV footage. He would like to have done it much sooner but unfortunately his tech expert and the hotel head of security were away on their annual vacation.

'Morning, Chris, morning, Rubin, all the best for 2020.'

'And to you,' they replied in unison.

'Jeremy not coming?' enquired Chris.

'Something came up. Right, let's get going. Start the footage at the 11.30 p.m. marker on the Saturday. I want to see if the couple from accounts leave.'

Chris scrolled forward until a car with two women pulled up at the exit point. The timer showed 11.46 p.m. The data confirmed they were indeed the couple of interest.

'Can you now jump ahead to 12.55 a.m. on the Sunday, I want to see if our lone woman leaves,' said Gary.

Chris scrolled forward again until a car stopped at the exit point with a lone woman driver. It was 1.04 a.m., nine minutes after she entered the elevator. The footage showed the security guard handing her the exit register and then scanning her identity document.

'Okay, Chris, that's exactly what I'm after. Let's look at that scanned ID.'

Bingo, there it was on record, the name of the lone woman. A crosscheck with the register confirmed her to be Carol Ibbets from Plaistowe's.

'A moment please, Chris, I need to make a quick call to Lucy.'

'We've got the name of our lone woman,' he announced excitedly. 'Carol Ibbets. It doesn't ring a bell with me. Do you know her?'

'She's one of David Plaistowe's personal assistants— only been with the firm about six months.'

'How well do you know her? Would you be able to ask her whether she saw or heard anything unusual in the parking basement?'

'We've chatted a few times and eaten lunch together occasionally, but I don't know her well. Let me see what I can do.'

'Sorry about that, Chris, a call I had to make. Let's look at the entry footage from 7 p.m. on the Saturday until the police arrive.'

After grinding their way through an exhausting and tedious day, they took stock over a quick bite at a nearby restaurant. Gary had managed to log the arrival and departure times of each car, as well as registration numbers, and Chris had downloaded a screengrab of the associated scanned ID. For the sake of completeness, Gary had also crosschecked the information with the register.

'Thanks so much for all your help, Chris. Identifying the lone woman was an absolute win. My instincts tell me she's going to become vitally important as the investigation rolls on.'

The following morning Gary's body clock woke him earlier than usual, in time to enjoy the sunrise from the seclusion of his bedroom balcony. Within minutes of the golden glow breaking the eastern horizon, its warmth consoled him. 'Hey, Charlie, what a beautiful day. What do you reckon, ready for your walk?'

The dog immediately jumped up on his hind legs and, with cocked ears, wagging tail and a panting, broad smile, rested his front paws against Gary's thigh in anticipation.

'Okay, come, a quick one, I've got a ton of stuff to do today.'

By late afternoon he had managed to get through all the captured data in his search for further clues. He glanced at his watch and knew he had enough time to visit Jeremy without being caught in heavy traffic. To his delight he found a more relaxed Jeremy, seemingly in control of his emotions. The haggard look of the last few weeks was all but gone. Jeremy led him towards the conservatory where drinks and snacks were already laid out on a corner table.

Jeremy stopped and turned. 'Any chance we can get rid of this bracelet and have my reporting conditions relaxed? It's a pain having to cover up whenever I go out, and damn inconvenient to schlepp to the police station every day.'

Gary carried on walking. 'Too early, but when it looks right, we'll push for changes.' He paused at one end of the sunny room to admire the huge colourful arrangement of stargazer lilies before bending over them to allow their heady scent to tickle his nostrils.

Setting down his drink, Gary withdrew some notes from a briefcase, ready to share the information Jeremy had been waiting for. 'I have here,' he said, 'a summary of people movements in and out of the hotel's parkade and down to the parking basements on the Saturday night and early Sunday morning.'

Jeremy, sitting forward, cut in impatiently. 'Anything significant or helpful?'

'I think so,' said Gary, 'but we need to follow up on a few things. Let me run through some of what we've discovered. At eleven thirty on Saturday night you and Amanda left the party, taking the elevator to the fifth parking basement where the police found you in the early hours of Sunday. The couple who got in the elevator with you didn't hang around and left the parkade shortly after you guys got off at the fifth. They've already been interviewed by the police but refuse to speak to us.'

'What did they say to the cops?' asked Jeremy, scratching his head.

'Don't know—we'll find out when we see the police docket.'

Gary paused, pushing a savoury biscuit into his mouth before taking another sip of scotch. Jeremy's eyes remained on him.

'At forty minutes past midnight Roger Plaistowe and two couples shared an elevator to the third parking basement. After another forty minutes, Roger caught the elevator on the third and returned to the lobby area. I'll come back to him in a moment.'

'Forty minutes unaccounted for,' said Jeremy. 'I suppose he could've gone to his car and then changed his mind about leaving, either because he was too drunk to drive or because he wanted to carry on partying.'

'You may well be right, but forty minutes is a long time,' said Gary. 'For reasons I'll touch on later, we need to look into his movements a lot more closely. Anyway, there are a couple of other people whose movements are of interest. Shortly before one in the morning, about fourteen minutes after Roger went down to the third basement, Carol Ibbets, one of David Plaistowe's personal assistants, took an elevator on her own to the fifth parking basement. Did she perhaps see or hear anything unusual? We don't yet know. She drove out of the parkade nine minutes later.'

'Shouldn't we be talking to her?' asked Jeremy.

Jeremy pushed the snacks towards Gary. 'These are delicious,' said Gary, biting into a slice of rye bread with salmon before responding.

'We plan to, don't you worry. I've asked Lucy to see whether she can broach the subject discreetly with her. Lucy doesn't know her all that well, so we might have to find another way. She may also have made a statement to the police.'

'What happens to Roger after his return to the lobby?' asked Jeremy.

'Well, before we go there, it's worth mentioning that at one twenty-five—that's five minutes after Roger returns from the basement—Bagley-Smith takes the elevator on his own to the fifth basement. There's no record of his car leaving before the police arrive and nothing on the CCTV showing his return to the lobby. It's possible he took the stairs back up to the lobby. The camera covering the door between the lobby and the stairwell was broken.'

'He's a creepy fellow,' said Jeremy.

Mrs Winters popped in to check if they needed anything. 'Who is this creepy fellow?' she asked.

'One of the partners who was in the hotel basement while I was down there—a horrible man, skinny, balding, rounded shoulders and piggy eyes. There's also a tight connection between him and the chairperson. And he also happened to be Amanda's boss.'

'Thanks for checking, Mrs Winters, but we've enough food here to last a week, and yummy, I have to say.'

Gary suspected that she wanted to stay but thought better of it.

'Anyway, I need to look into his comings and goings a bit more,' said Gary. 'I want to find out how long he stayed in the basement and what he was up to.

'Back to our friend Roger. He disappeared out of sight after coming up from the basement, but thirty-five minutes later at 1.55 a.m. he returned with his father. As far as we can judge from the footage, both appeared agitated. They immediately took the elevator, not to the third parking basement, however, but to the fifth. Remember, previously Roger went down to the third and returned from the third. I have to ask, why to the fifth?'

Gary sat back, waiting for Jeremy to digest the information.

'There could be any number of innocent explanations, I guess', offered Jeremy. 'Any movement by them after that?'

'Sure,' said Gary, 'but I would at some point like to hear their explanations. There was further movement. The footage marker shows that at 2.06 a.m. David left the building, driving his car. He was accompanied by Roger.'

'There we are—the innocent explanation,' said Jeremy. 'Roger's too drunk to drive his own car. He does the responsible thing and calls on the old man to take him home and off they go.'

'But why from the fifth basement? There's no way David Plaistowe parked that far down,' said Gary. 'And here's another interesting thing, fifty-two minutes later David returns to the hotel, apparently on his own.

According to the entrance register he returned to fetch his mobile, which he says he had left behind. That sounds plausible but for one thing. He would've had to return to the lobby area from the basement. There's no evidence from the CCTV footage of him doing so.'

'Is there no other way he could have returned without being spotted by the cameras?'

'He could've taken the stairs, but I think that's unlikely given the time. Why would he take the stairs when the elevator would have been more convenient? He's not a young man.'

They sat in silence for a few minutes pondering the situation. 'One for the road, Gary?' asked Jeremy, walking to the drinks table.

'A single.'

'What time did David Plaistowe finally leave?' enquired Jeremy.

'At 3.12.a.m. According to the police, the attack on Amanda happened before three thirty on Sunday morning,' said Gary.

'If after his return David parked in the basement closest to the ground floor it wouldn't have been unusual for him to take the stairs,' said Jeremy. 'He might have been nervous of being trapped in the elevator at that time. I would be, that's for certain.'

'That's possible, but it smells a bit fishy.'

'What about all the others who went down to the parking basements?'

'All accounted for. They left the parkade within ten minutes of taking the elevator.'

'So where to from here?'

'To chat to Carol Ibbets in the hope she may have seen or heard something. I'm also expecting the forensic results any day now. Hopefully they will reveal something useful. And I want to look more closely into Bagley-Smith's movements.'

'When do we get to see the police docket?' queried Jeremy.

'We're allowed copies once their investigations are complete.'

'And how do we know when they reach that point?'

'If and when you're formally charged, we can assume their investigations are done.'

'What about the prosecution witnesses? Can we interview them?'

'Yes, if they agree, but the prosecutor must be invited to attend.'

'I can't see Bagley-Smith and the Plaistowes agreeing,' said Jeremy.

'Let's wait and see.'

They were interrupted by Jeremy's ringing phone. He answered it, leapt up from his chair and headed quickly to the door with a broad smile. 'It's Lucy,' he mouthed silently.

He returned a few minutes later with a slight skip. 'Sorry about that but I couldn't ignore her call. Where were we? Oh yes, I know what I wanted to say—it seems we haven't yet got much to go on. I'm worried.'

'We have a way to go,' admitted Gary, 'but there are a few chinks. Something's not quite right in the movements of Roger and his father, and of Bagley-Smith, I can't figure it out right now, but I will in time. It's a slow process, my mate—and one that gives up only a little bit at a time.'

'I guess you're right. I lie awake at night fretting about how this is going to end.'

'Before I forget, here's a copy of Professor East's final opinion,' said Gary. 'Much as we expected—he doesn't think your claim of amnesia is a crock, given the amount of booze you drank on top of the meds. He also says, most importantly, that if a person has a blackout it's not unusual that he or she believes the blackout events didn't happen.'

'That's good for us hey, Gary?'

'Definitely, but as I said before, you'd still have to give convincing evidence under cross examination.'

'I know. There must be at least twenty witnesses we can call to substantiate how much I drank and how drunk I was.'

'Agreed. Anyway, what did the beautiful young Lucy want?'

Jeremy allowed himself an indulgent smile. 'She is beautiful, isn't she? She's coming to visit me on Sunday morning. Why don't you come around at about twelve for a braai? I've invited some of the Plaistowe crowd who've been supportive.'

'Sounds good.'

9

The leisurely Saturday morning in bed brought Gary a welcome, albeit short, reprieve from the frustrating challenges of the last six weeks. He was looking forward to the barbecue the following day and meeting up with some of the old friends that he hadn't seen for a while.

Although his work on Jeremy's case had almost ground to a halt because of police and forensic lab delays, he felt mentally and physically sapped and badly in need of a holiday. Besides being consumed by his friend's crisis—both legal and psychological—he had his own family turmoil to cope with. His mother, a dear, gentle soul, was struggling to come to terms with the fact that she was close to becoming a widow after forty years of marriage. She and Gary's father, now home on palliative care, had for most of their married life been inseparable. The mounting expenses for cancer treatment brought additional pressure as his parents' modest savings were fast running out. His sister was in no position to help, so the burden fell on him. Stepping up to help wasn't in itself a burden—the issue was his own financial constraints. When he realised that the case would be protracted, he had taken out a second mortgage on his home to tide him over until he could arrange alternative employment. That had helped but the proceeds too would run out in the next few months. Hopefully it wouldn't be too long before he could start earning an income again.

The passing of his father would leave a massive hole in their lives. He was a loving, reliable and dependable husband, and devoted father, and never too busy to help or listen and, when sought, to give wise advice. He had been Gary's inspirational role model and hero and someone he deeply admired and respected. His mantra was to stand up for the truth always, even if it entailed sacrifice or disadvantage. Now Gary understood firsthand what he had meant.

Mrs Edwards and her daughter were wilting under the stress of seeing him wither away and suffer the ugly side effects of chemotherapy. More and more they leaned on Gary for support. For Mr Edwards senior, life's journey was nearing the end; he could no longer tolerate the pain, nausea and indignity. The time had come to let go, to stop the treatment and let his disease win. He had known it for some time; now the Edwards family had to accept it too.

Noticing the time, Gary jumped out of bed and made his way hastily downstairs, followed by an excited Charlie. He grabbed a bowl of muesli, berries and yoghurt and took it to the sunny verandah. Charlie remained standing at his feet, staring up expectantly, and only when Gary said nothing about going for a walk, did he lie down, chin on front paws.

'I know, I know, Charlie, you're disappointed. I'm sorry but it's a bit of a rush today, I'm afraid. I'll make it up to you, I promise.'

Charlie blinked those large brown eyes as if to say he understood.

Not being able to dawdle any longer he skipped his shower, threw on tennis kit, and dashed out of the door, arriving at the tennis club with five minutes to spare. Grabbing his togs and racquet from the boot, he rushed into the clubhouse, waving to Pillay who was already into his first match.

After a strenuous morning of tough matches, Gary caught up with the young detective. 'Great tennis, Dhanraj, you played well today—striking the ball sweetly. You've been working on that backhand drop shot I see.'

'Thanks, Gary, you didn't do so badly yourself. How're you doing?'

'Mm, a bit tough going these last few weeks. My father's terribly ill and is back home, having decided to stop chemo,' said Gary with a grimace.

'Sorry to hear that.'

'We're all destined to die but that doesn't stop the pain or grief, hey? I've also been a bit frustrated, waiting for the forensic results and for you guys to wrap up so I can go through the police docket.'

Dhanraj hesitated and then walked over to the drinks table helping himself to another bottle of water.

Gary sensed something unsaid. 'And how have you been?' he asked.

'Not too bad, at least no family issues.'

'I sense a "but" there. What's up?' asked Gary, stepping closer.

'Sometimes the job gets to me. Kumalo's a difficult guy to work for—wants everything done his way,' he said, rolling his eyes with a slight shake of the head. 'And that temper, oh boy, it gets ugly at times.'

'I tried to get hold of him yesterday, but with no luck,' commented Gary.

'I'm not surprised. He's away on some fancy hunting trip and only back on Tuesday. Others have told me he's a great cop, and that he always plays his cards close to his chest.'

'Have you found that?'

'I have, particularly on the Egoli Hotel case. He simply won't let me follow my own leads. Every little thing has to go through him. And, and, he seems to be mistrusting of his team, always locking his office when he leaves, even just to go to the bathroom.'

'That must be frustrating as hell for you.'

'Look, I don't mind having to clear follow-ups with him—some guys are control freaks, I get that. But—' Pillay stopped.

'But what?' asked Gary.

'I think I've said too much already. My apologies. I shouldn't be talking out of school.'

'Hey, Dhanraj, we're mates. You can let off a bit of steam and you know you can trust me.'

Pillay plonked himself down, resting his size twelve tennis shoes over a plastic chair. Gary drew up another chair.

'It's frustrating that sometimes he blocks things for no good reason. Leads that should obviously be got after.'

'Why don't you stand up to him?'

'Not a chance, he won't put up with it and would make my life hell. He's also the sort of boss who can either make or break one's career.'

Gary sensed there was more but figured that if he wanted to get information from Pillay about the case it would be best not to probe the relationship—at least not for the moment.

'Bosses can be difficult,' sympathised Gary. 'You should try working under a chairperson like David

Plaistowe. Now there's a difficult sod if ever there was one. Anyway, enough about the bosses. We've picked up a few funnies from the CCTV footage and hotel parkade registers.'

'I thought you might,' said Pillay. 'I bet they're the same ones we've noticed.'

Gary outlined the unusual movements of the Plaistowes, father and son, and Bagley-Smith.

'But why don't you track their mobile phone movements and even their car movements?' suggested Gary. 'You guys have the authority, and my guess is their cars are all fitted with tracking devices.'

'This is one of those follow-ups that Kumalo sees as a complete waste of time and money,' said Pillay. 'He sees no benefit and is adamant the case against Winters will be a walkover.'

'Does that mean you've already got all the forensic reports and lab results?'

'No, but Kumalo's confident, as am I, I have to say, what they'll confirm.'

'I was hoping I would be saved the trouble of following up on movements,' said Gary. 'There's something terribly wrong here, but for the moment I can't put my finger on it. I think we could learn a lot from their mobile phone and car movements.'

'Possibly.'

'For us it means trying to get a court order to force the mobile phone companies and vehicle tracking companies to make their records and data available for analysis. It's going to take time and will cost a packet, and there's no guarantee the court will give us an order. Can't you push harder with Kumalo?'

'Believe me I've tried, all I got was a roasting second to none.'

'What explanations have these guys given?' enquired Gary.

'I don't want to be difficult, Gary, but I think I've said enough. Please understand.'

'I take it you know the camera covering the door to the stairs from the lobby area was broken?'

'The hotel's G.M. mentioned that,' said Pillay looking at his watch. 'Hey, Gary, good to catch up but I need to dash.'

'It's been good. Don't let Kumalo bully you. Cover your arse so nothing comes back to bite you. You're a fine detective with a fantastic record.'

By the time Gary arrived home and jumped in the shower it was already past lunchtime. Feeling like a bite and a good movie (and perhaps more) he called an engaging new friend: the winsome swimwear model, Julia.

'Are none of the others available?' she asked with feigned pique.

'Don't know what you mean.'

'Aren't I your last resort go-to girl?'

He roared with laughter. 'C'mon, Jules, you know that's not true. You're the first one I called, promise.'

'I'll need some convincing, *Mr Edwards*, but sure, that'll be fun. Give me thirty minutes.'

Although they dated periodically, neither of them sought a serious relationship, mainly because of career demands. But today, all thoughts of work were sidelined. He put all his thoughts to romancing a beautiful woman.

Rarely did Gary have the opportunity to laze two mornings in a row. The early church bells didn't bother him this Sunday; it hadn't been a late night because of Julia's early flight to the Seychelles for a photo shoot.

He heard Charlie grunting and snorting his way up the stairs to the master bedroom. Charlie took off as soon as he entered the room, running as fast as his short legs could carry him, and jumped onto the bed.

'Howzit, my old pal, how're you this fine morning? Sleep well?' Gary flung his arms around Charlie and turned him on his back to tickle his belly. The dog kicked his legs furiously, growling playfully and trying to catch Gary's hands in huge, gaping jaws.

'You like that, don't you,' he said in a teasing tone reserved for Charlie as he intensified the tickling. Suddenly Gary moved away, pinching his nose and letting go of the excited staffie. 'Oh no, Charlie, that's unsociable—what've you been eating?' Charlie flipped onto his tummy, chin on front paws, and peered at Gary intermittently. Gary lay back on his interlocked hands tucked behind his head and beckoned his little friend who crept over next to him, giving a satisfied grunt.

'You know, I had such a good time yesterday with Julia—you know, the tall, beautiful model.' Charlie cocked his ears, appearing to be listening to every word. 'I like her—she's great fun—we laugh at the same things and enjoy doing the same things... hey, are you listening? This is important stuff.'

Charlie sat up and stared at Gary, tilting his head from side to side. 'That's better, much better. Here's the thing though—she thinks I only call her when I'm desperate.' Charlie grunted again. 'That's not true, I like her the best. Maybe more than anyone I've met in recent years...' He leaned over and rubbed Charlie's head.

'I know that look, you want to go for a walk.' At the mention of the word, Charlie leapt off the bed and aimed for the door with a wagging tail.

They slipped out of the backyard gate onto a path which led to a public park where Charlie could run freely off his leash. After an hour they returned home, Charlie well satisfied, having done all the usual things —marking his territory on more bushes than Gary cared to count, storming at the occasional plover with no chance of inflicting any damage, then cooling down in the shallow waters of a stream while baring his teeth at any intruder in his space.

Decisions, decisions. Breakfast at his favourite deli down the road or in the comfort of his own home? He flicked the kettle switch before finding something suitable in the refrigerator. The morning slipped away. When he thought to cast his eyes over to the clock, he thought he'd better phone. The call went to voice mail.

'Hi, Jeremy, before you say anything, I know, I know, I'm late. Sorry. I'm leaving in five. See you.'

The smell of wood smoke wafted over his car on the approach to the Winters' home. Some of his former colleagues, dressed casually in tee shirts, shorts and sneakers, gathered in small groups close to the open fires. Gary couldn't help noticing Jeremy's arm dangling over Lucy's bare shoulders. She looked smashing in a skimpy summer outfit, showing off her petite figure and shapely tanned legs.

'Punched anyone recently?' shouted a friend.

'Late night with the swimwear model?' came another.

'Who are these people?' asked Gary of no one in particular. 'Presumably not friends?' He laughed and joined the groups in turn, shaking hands, kissing cheeks, and slapping backs. 'So good to see you all.'

He reached out to Jeremy with a sincere man hug, at the same time extending a hand to Lucy. 'Hi guys, sorry I'm late, I couldn't get going this morning.'

'It must've been that model!' chirped another friend.

'I've no idea what you're talking about,' said Gary.

'Come, come, Gary, no need to be shy about moving in celebrity circles, I saw you at the Hyde Park movies yesterday.'

'She's a friend, nothing more.'

The ragging persisted for a good while before Jeremy banged a dinner gong. 'Listen up, guys. Thanks for making the effort today and most importantly, thank you for your wonderful support during this time. And—' he paused '—a special thanks to my oldest and closest friend, and also your good friend, Gary, for standing by me in this fight; a fight we're going to win... because I'm *innocent.*'

Everyone showed their agreement with loud applause and affirmed their ongoing support.

Jeremy banged the gong again. 'It's time for *shisa nyama,* so help yourselves to meat and get going. If you haven't worked it out yet, the orange drum is low heat and the other, hot intense heat.'

Everybody grabbed a plate and headed for the food. Gary stepped up to Lucy in the queue. 'Any luck with our lone woman?'

'Not yet. She's away on a hunting trip with her boss until Tuesday.'

'Say that again,' replied Gary, not believing his ears.

'David Plaistowe has taken a group of VIPs to his hunting lodge and his assistants have gone along to help out. They left on Friday on a chartered flight.'

'That's most interesting,' said Gary, choosing a thick piece of ribeye.

'Why?' she asked, helping herself to a small fillet.

Jeremy mingled with his guests, making sure they had what they needed and then joined Gary and Lucy at the fire.

'You're in time to hear something interesting,' said Lucy, turning her gaze to Gary.

'I saw Pillay at tennis yesterday morning and he told me Kumalo was away from Friday until Tuesday on some fancy hunting trip,' said Gary.

'And so?' queried Jeremy with a furrowed brow.

'Well, Lucy has told me she hasn't been able to speak to our lone woman from the CCTV footage because she and Plaistowe's other assistants are helping out on a hunting trip that he's hosting at his lodge—wait for it—from Friday to Tuesday.'

Lucy started to ask something, but Jeremy got in first. 'Do you think Kumalo's on that trip?'

'It would be a helluva coincidence if he's on a different hunting trip,' remarked Lucy.

'For sure,' joined in Gary. 'I wonder what that's all about. A detective is not the sort of guest Plaistowe would take on a weekend like that.'

'He's definitely not one for fraternising with the hoi polloi,' added Jeremy.

'You're so right; he's too much of a snob,' agreed Gary. 'I'll do some sniffing about. Anyway, come, it's time to kick back.'

The weekend turned out better and more relaxing than Gary expected. He was pleased to see that the party had lifted Jeremy's spirits. Saturday hadn't been too bad either—the first of two lie-ins, some competitive tennis, constructive engagement with Pillay, and to top off the day, a lovely time with Julia. Gary revelled in the fact that he had been spotted with one of the most beautiful models in the country. The word was out, which somehow made their relationship less frivolous.

Even though he was free from the routine of having to rush to the office early on Monday mornings, Gary still experienced those blues that always seemed to visit at the beginning of a new week. It took a concerted effort to shake off an uncomfortable feeling of dread in the pit of his stomach and settle himself in the study. He thought about the case and the way forward, anticipating that forensics would confirm the presence of Jeremy's DNA in Amanda's vaginal swabs and fingernail scrapings. He also expected that the fingerprints on the champagne bottle were theirs. He sat back and looked up at the ceiling, wondering what the couple from accounts had said in their police interview. *I hope there isn't a nasty little surprise waiting for us.*

He weighed up the probative value of these considerations in light of the other known facts: the obscure position of Jeremy's car; the location of Amanda's body in a rarely used stairwell in close proximity to the car; Jeremy's denial of intimacy with Amanda during the party; and his denial that Amanda accompanied him when he left the party.

Gary was worried. But on the other hand there was Professor East's supporting opinion. If Jeremy stood up well when giving evidence, the opinion would neutralise his denials to the police. And rape wasn't the only inference that could be drawn from the presence of his DNA.

He doodled on his legal pad, reflecting on matters that could tip the scales in favour of the prosecution. Unless the lone woman or the couple from accounts implicate Jeremy in some manner, the prosecution would have to prove two things. First, that none of those people, such as the Plaistowes and Bagley-Smith, who had known access to the fifth basement, could have been the perpetrators, and, secondly, that no other person could have gained access to the fifth basement without being seen.

On the first point, Bagley-Smith and the Plaistowes would have to testify and give credible innocent explanations for their time in the basements. He would have to wait to see the police docket to learn what they had to say.

Because of the broken CCTV camera that covered the door to the stairway, he figured the second point could be problematic for the prosecution. He wondered how anyone could disprove the reasonable possibility of a potential perpetrator using the door adjacent to the elevators. Despite some flaws in the case against

Jeremy, Gary wasn't bullish enough to leave matters there. Given the sexually charged interaction between him and Amanda when they almost fell into the elevator, it seemed highly probable that she was a consenting party. *There has to be exculpatory evidence somewhere and I need to find it.*

He scribbled some action points: *The lone woman; Analyse and test forensic reports; Examine dress; PI onto Kumalo/Plaistowe; Police docket/interview prosecution witnesses.*

Rubin was, as always, courteous and accommodating and offered to meet with Gary in the afternoon. 'Allow me to buy you lunch, Rubin. I'm sure you know Mario's around the corner from your office.'

'Are you sure? I don't want to put you out.'

'Absolutely. You're doing me a favour. I want to check a couple of points on security. Won't take long. Will one o'clock work for you?'

'See you then.'

Rubin ordered spaghetti alla puttanesca, Gary, penne arrabbiata. They settled on still water rather than alcohol.

'How can I help?' asked Rubin, waving to someone on the other side of the restaurant.

'I'm a bit stuck on one thing concerning people movements on the night or morning of Amanda Shelton's murder. If I understood correctly when last we spoke, a person could access the parking basements in one of three ways—by elevator from the elevator lobby area or by stairs from that lobby or via the parkade entrance. Correct?'

'Correct.'

'No other way?'

'Definitely not.'

'Over the weekend of our party the CCTV camera covering the door to the stairs was broken the entire time. Correct?'

'Yes, correct.'

'I know the CCTV cameras covering the elevators as well as the entrance and exit points in and out of the parkade were working. Given the broken camera, I assume a person who was already in the hotel could have gone down the stairs to the basements without being caught on camera?'

'Yes. The elevator cameras are arced in such a way they only pick up movement immediately in front of the elevator doors and into the elevators when the doors are open.'

'Is the rest of the elevator lobby area not covered by a camera?'

'It is normally, but that camera functioned off the same circuit as the one covering the doorway to the stairs, so it too was also out of order.'

Gary pondered the issue while the waiter served their meal. 'Okay, I now understand. So, the whole of the elevator lobby area, except immediately in front of the elevator doors, was uncovered?'

'Yes, you're right. But of course only a few people would have known that.'

'Good point,' said Gary, continuing with his questions while they ate. 'If someone wanted to enter or leave the hotel other than via the parkade entrance or exit, how would they do that?'

'There are only two ways,' said Rubin. 'Through the front doors, that's the glass revolving door and the door next to it, or via the staff entrance. The staff entrance requires a security card to be swiped each time a person wants to come in or leave and the swipe is captured on our digital security system.'

'I take it the front doors, as well as the main hotel foyer, are covered by cameras?'

'Certainly, and they were over the weekend of your party.'

'Besides people from our party, what sort of numbers are we looking at in terms of people coming and going through the front doors and crossing the main foyer, between say seven thirty on the Saturday night and three on the Sunday?'

'Many hundreds. We have six bars and eight restaurants in the hotel. You can imagine the activity.'

'It seems it would've been quite easy for some unknown person to slip down to basement five, rape and kill Amanda, and exit the hotel without being identified?'

'Theoretically you're right. But why would he, and how would he even know where Miss Shelton was?'

'I take your point. It's more likely that it would have been someone at our party who had his eye on her and when he had his way, he could have left through the front doors.'

'We know Miss Shelton was attacked somewhere between eleven thirty and three so why don't you review the footage that covers the foyer and front doors to check which men from your firm left at that time.'

'There would be too many, but I'll bear this in mind when we have the results of the DNA samples taken by the police from all the young men in the firm

10

The incoming call interrupted Gary's thoughts on how best to unravel David Plaistowe's relationship with Captain Kumalo, assuming they were on the same hunting trip.

'Howzit, Lucy. All well?'

'All good, and you?'

'Strong as always. You and Jeremy seemed to be hitting it off on Sunday.'

'I enjoyed the time. But still early days.'

'You guys are a perfect match, but, hey, I'm all for taking time on matters of the heart,' said Gary.

'I don't want to rush things, particularly at this time; Jeremy's extremely vulnerable and now needs close friends more than a girlfriend. Anyway, enough about that. The reason for calling is that I had a chat with Carol Ibbets at lunch today.'

'And?'

'Well, I learned she got her position with David through her father. Apparently, he and David go back a long way. They're good friends, and also have some common business interests in the mining industry.'

'Go on.'

'But here's the other interesting thing. Captain Kumalo *was* on the hunting trip, as was his wife. According to Carol there were sixteen guests, mainly politicians and businesspeople.'

'Did she tell you the purpose of the trip?'

'Networking and schmoozing.'

'Anything else?' asked Gary expectantly.

'No, nothing important. She didn't volunteer, and I didn't want to pry—too early. I want to build some rapport with her. I talked a bit about Amanda and how some of us can't believe—*don't* believe—that Jeremy killed her.'

'And her reaction?'

'She changed the subject rather abruptly and suddenly appeared a bit nervous—you know, avoiding eye contact and biting on a fingernail, that sort of thing. From what I've seen of her before, she's not the nervy type.'

'I agree, don't push—gently, gently will work better. We've got time. Carol might be our trump card. Onto something else: what's your take on Jeremy's emotional state?'

'I'm no expert but we spent a lot of time talking on Sunday and we had supper together last night, and he seemed stronger. He takes enormous comfort having you by his side. Bottom line, I sensed a more positive Jeremy. He's convinced evidence will come out proving his innocence.'

'That's good to hear. I think he's over the initial shock and now understands the process, but let's not forget Professor East's caution.'

'I haven't. I'll keep in touch every day. His folks and I are on the same page. What lovely people.'

'Salt of the earth. I'll also keep up my daily contact with him. Thanks for the call. Chat later and good luck with Carol.'

His thoughts returned to Kumalo and Plaistowe. The hunting trip may be a red herring, but his niggling instincts suggested otherwise. He snatched up his phone and searched for Willem Snyman's number. Before becoming a private investigator some fifteen years back, Willem was already a seasoned detective with more than twenty years' service in the South African police force. In their many past cases Gary found him to be top notch, discreet and thorough. He often succeeded where others failed.

He answered on the second ring. 'Still keeping crooks out of jail?' he asked with a chortle. 'How the hell are you? It's been a while.'

'All well, and you? Still sneaking around the Cayman Islands, Mauritius, Cyprus and other exotic places hunting for ill-gotten gains?'

'Don't joke, my friend, the country's being bled dry. I seem to be spending more time out of the country trying to get to grips with the nefarious activities of some of our finest,' said Snyman, pausing for a moment. 'Our finest tax cheats, crooked businessmen, and husbands hiding their wealth from former wives.'

'And that's why you're so qualified for this next little assignment I have for you. If this is a bad time we can chat later.'

'Fire away, I'm all ears.'

Gary asked whether he had come across Captain Kumalo.

'Is that Thabani Kumalo, quite a big man in his early forties—suave, natty dresser?'

'Sounds like him.'

'There was a junior detective by that name in our Commercial Crimes Unit for about a year before I left the force. I didn't know him well personally, but by all accounts he was a capable officer and quite ambitious. What's your interest in him?'

Gary sketched in the background to the case, not overlooking Kumalo's apparent reticence to allowing Pillay a degree of freedom in the investigation. 'I need to find out whether there's any corrupt relationship between Kumalo and Plaistowe. There's something here that doesn't smell quite right.'

'It does seem odd,' said the P.I., 'that someone as elite and as wealthy as Plaistowe would socialise with a career policeman, especially one heading up the investigation. I guess there's the possibility it's a P.R. exercise.'

'What do you mean?' asked Gary.

'Plaistowe wanting the firm's clients to know he's encouraging and supporting Kumalo in his search for the truth.'

'Mm, that would be stretching things, but hey, let's see what you come up with. Happy with the usual fee and expense arrangements?'

'Of course. I'll do some preliminary digging over the next week or so and get back to you. And thanks for the work—always appreciated.'

Finally, the following morning, the news he had been waiting for: the forensic test results were in. Pillay said Captain Kumalo wanted to meet with Jeremy at their offices. Gary's prying drew a hasty rebuke from Pillay who refused to be drawn.

'Don't be late Gary, two o'clock sharp. The captain's in one of his crotchety moods.'

Instead of phoning the Winters, he took off for their home in his Ferrari. Jeremy's father greeted him cheerily at the front door, wiping at the dirty smudge across his right cheek with a gloved hand.

'You've caught me in my gardening kit,' he chuckled. 'Let me call the gang.'

Before Gary could give any sort of forewarning, Mr Winters ducked into the adjacent guest cloakroom at the same time hollering for his wife and son. They rushed down the stairs to the front door.

'Come in, come in,' beckoned a breathless Mrs Winters, hairbrush in hand. 'I'll pop the kettle on.'

'I won't have anything, thanks Mrs Winters. I'm afraid I'm in a bit of a rush.'

As soon as Mr Winters, now free of the gardening gloves and dirty smudge, joined them, Gary conveyed the gist of his earlier conversation with Pillay. 'I've little doubt they're going to ask Jeremy some more questions in light of the forensic results. I also suspect they'll announce he's to be formally charged.'

Wincing, Mrs Winters brought a shaking hand up to her mouth, dropping the hairbrush to clatter on the tiled floor. She glanced at Jeremy, then at her husband and finally at Gary. Her husband shifted closer to her on the couch, placing his right arm gently across her shoulders and pulling her in towards himself.

Surprisingly, Jeremy seemed calm. 'This shouldn't come as a surprise. We've known the police were waiting for forensic confirmation which they now seem to have. I know I didn't harm Amanda. I'm innocent and have nothing to fear.'

Jeremy's sudden grimace and rubbing of his chest didn't escape Gary's attention.

'Jeremy's right, Mrs Winters. We'll go and hear what they have to say, but I won't let him answer any questions or make any comments. I might have some questions of my own for them depending on what we learn. This isn't unusual, so don't be alarmed. The evidence is circumstantial, and we're far from done with our investigations. Our plan is to destroy their case.'

For a moment, his words rang hollow in his ears and he wondered if the others harboured as many doubts.

'What happens next?' asked Mr Winters, still comforting his wife. 'Will Jeremy remain out on bail?'

'If the DPP decides to indict to the High Court, Jeremy will, when he next appears in the Magistrates Courts, be remanded to appear in the High Court for the setting of a trial date,' replied Gary.

'And bail?' asked Mrs Winters.

'I can't imagine the State will ask for a remand in custody; nothing's happened since his last appearance to justify the scrapping of bail.'

'I know I've asked before, but can't we now have my bail conditions relaxed?' asked Jeremy. 'The bracelet and daily reporting are getting to me.'

'We'll try. You might get away with one of those but not both,' said Gary.

'If I have a choice, I'd prefer to avoid the daily reporting.'

'Okay, understood. I need to run. Will call for you at one o'clock.'

On time, Kumalo sauntered into the cold, poky interview room, with a slight nod of his neatly groomed head in the direction of Jeremy and Gary. As he took his place next to Pillay, he peered towards the side table to check the recording equipment had been switched on. Jeremy shivered slightly—the memories of his last visit to the room must have come flooding back. Gary patted him lightly on the leg to remind him he was not alone in the fight. Thankfully, the brutish Constable Jansen was nowhere in sight, no doubt nervous of another confrontation with Gary.

Kumalo brusquely disposed of the preliminaries, announcing the date, time and place of the meeting and the identities of those present, and reminded Jeremy of his constitutional rights.

'Well, here we are on 15 January 2020, and we have the forensic test results,' he said. 'Much quicker than normal, hey, Mr Edwards? I want to go over some of those with you.'

He wasted little time, electing, no doubt deliberately, to start with the most damning evidence first.

'Semen found in the victim's vagina came from you, Mr Winters, as did skin scrapings from under her fingernails.' He paused for what felt like an unnecessarily long time. 'What do you have to say about that?' His eyes bored into Jeremy.

'My client declines to comment at this stage,' said Gary. He had a good idea what was coming next.

'The panties found in your jacket pocket belonged to Miss Shelton and the blood on the champagne bottle found next to her body also came from her. Any comment?' asked Kumalo, again locking eyes with his suspect.

'No comment,' responded Gary.

Kumalo and Pillay looked at each other before Kumalo charged ahead. 'The only fingerprints on the champagne bottle were yours and Miss Shelton's. Quite clearly, she didn't assault herself, so what do you have to say about that?'

'Were there any fingerprints on the neck of the bottle?' asked Gary.

Kumalo looked down, shuffling some papers. 'No, only on the bulge. What do you say about that, Mr Winters?'

'He has no comment, but I do. It seems the neck has been wiped clean. Why would my client wipe the neck clean and not the rest of the bottle?'

Smiling and tapping his pen on the table, Kumalo leaned back in his chair and ignored the question.

'So, let's see what we have. You, Mr Winters, are passed out, half naked, on the passenger seat of your car, parked in a dark corner of the fifth basement parking area. Miss Shelton's body is found in a stairwell close to your car. She has been raped and then strangled to death.' Kumalo's eyes flicked between Pillay, Jeremy and Gary. 'The victim's panties are in your jacket pocket, your semen (and only yours) is in her vagina, some of your skin is under Miss Shelton's fingernails, and your fingerprints are on the champagne bottle next to her body.'

He paused for effect.

'When we interviewed you, you categorically denied having had any intimate relations with the victim that night. In fact, you were insistent that you left the party alone. We now know that was a pack of lies.'

Kumalo's voice was raised and his upper lip twitched.

Jeremy opened his mouth to respond but Gary cut him short. 'As before, my client is exercising his right to remain silent.'

'We also have two witnesses who shared the elevator with you and Miss Shelton when you left the party, and they've told us that Miss Shelton was reluctant to get off at the fifth level and wanted to return to the party. According to them, you pulled her out of the elevator, insisting that she go to your car with you.'

Oh, my fuck this is not good, thought Gary.

'Detective Sergeant Pillay and I aren't the only ones who think the evidence against you is overwhelming.' He slid copies of the lab reports towards Gary, Kumalo's voice now booming. 'You see, the Director of Public Prosecutions had no hesitation in deciding to indict you for trial in the High Court on charges of rape and murder.'

Gary took his time reading the reports and then looked at Kumalo who propped up his chin in the palm of one hand. With the other hand he drew a stick figure behind prison bars on the pad in front of him.

'For the record, I have to ask, Captain Kumalo, why you're drawing that picture—a picture of a person behind prison bars?' questioned Gary.

'That's exactly where your client belongs,' snapped Kumalo, now writing the word "LIFE" in bold letters across the top of the sketch.

Gary looked at Jeremy and shook his head before continuing. 'I don't see any lab report on the victim's dress, and what about the DNA samples you took from all the other young men in the firm?'

'There was nothing of consequence to report. The lab found no stains, no evidence of any kind on the dress, and nothing to match the other samples. I'll get you a copy of that report on your way out. Is that it? Are you ready to leave, Mr Winters, to enjoy your last moments of freedom?'

'Don't you think it's odd there were no semen stains on the dress?' queried Gary. 'We know a condom wasn't used.'

'No, I don't. Mr Winters could have pulled the victim's dress up before raping her. Are you done, Mr Edwards?'

'Nearly, please bear with me. I would like our expert to inspect the dress.'

'Not a problem. Sergeant Pillay will liaise with you.'

'Thank you,' said Gary. 'At the next court appearance we intend asking that the bracelet and daily reporting requirements be dropped. I believe Mr Winters has demonstrated he's not a flight risk or likely to interfere with witnesses. How would you feel about that?'

'Not a chance.'

11

They had hardly pulled out of the courtyard before Jeremy grabbed Gary's left arm. 'Am... am... am I going to end up in custody?' stammered Jeremy. 'And what about the two witnesses who claimed I forced Amanda out of the elevator? I would never have done that. What's happening?'

'Calm down, one thing at a time. I don't believe you'll be remanded in custody, but we better have senior counsel there. I don't know what's got into Kumalo.'

'I hope you... you... you're right. It's another fi... five days before my court appearance. That's all I need hanging over my head now. Dammit! I've had it.'

Fearing Kumalo's performance would push Jeremy into a deep depression again, Gary pulled off the road and killed the motor. 'Look, pal, I've been involved in hundreds of bail applications and there's no way you're going into custody. He's trying to spook you. The man's a real jerk.'

Jeremy fiddled with his seatbelt and then with the air vents on his side and then he scratched his scalp repeatedly, casting glances in Gary's direction. This worried Gary; if Kumalo could shake Jeremy so easily, it wouldn't take much to rattle him on the witness stand.

'What about those two witnesses. If that's what they're going to say in court, I'm dead, I'll have no chance.'

'Let's see what they actually said in their statements and what the context was. Even though you can't remember them, I cannot believe you would've tried to force Amanda out of the elevator in front of others; that isn't plausible.'

'What did you think of the rest of the meeting?' asked Jeremy, wringing his hands and biting on his lip.

'Nothing new except for the absence of stains on the dress and the fact that the neck of the champagne bottle had been wiped clean. Why would you go to the trouble of getting rid of fingerprints on the neck and not bother with the rest of the bottle?'

'I'm not following.'

'I think the person who hit Amanda with the bottle knew he had held the bottle by its neck and that's why he wiped that part only.'

'And what about the dress?' asked Jeremy.

'As I said to Kumalo, it's odd that no stains were found. We know you didn't use a condom, so I was expecting a stained dress, even if only slightly, unless Amanda was completely naked. A bit unlikely, would be my guess. But even if she was, why no stain after she got dressed?'

They sat in silence, Jeremy frightened about his upcoming court appearance and Gary nervous about his pal going to pieces and the incriminating testimonies of the couple from accounts.

'I know Kumalo's unsettled you. Have you still got some of the anxiety meds and sleeping tablets?'

'Yes.'

'You've got to hold it together, Jeremy, so please take the meds.'

Gary dropped him off at his parent's home, reminding him again to take his meds.

As soon as Jeremy stepped out of the car, Gary called Lucy to let her know what had transpired.

'I think it'll be a good idea if I stay over at the Winters' home until the hearing is out of the way,' she said. 'I'll get hold of them after this call.'

'Good thinking.'

The sustained support from Lucy, friends and family, as well as the repeated reassurances from his formidable legal team, carried Jeremy through the following week. On the morning of the hearing he appeared calm as he tentatively ascended the steps of the court building, bolstered by his full legal team, his parents and Lucy.

Kumalo, Pillay and the prosecutor were in a huddle when the defence team entered the courtroom. The team leader approached the prosecutor and enquired whether she intended to follow through on Kumalo's threat.

'Captain Kumalo is firmly of the view that your client is a flight risk now that he has been formally charged, and thinks he should go back into custody,' she replied.

'That's absurd,' challenged Jeremy's senior counsel. 'The accused has behaved impeccably since his first court appearance many weeks ago and not once has he breached his bail conditions. He holds only one passport which has already been surrendered to the

Clerk of Court, he's lived in South Africa since birth, owns an apartment here, is employed, and his family live here. And furthermore, substantial bail has been posted.'

'I'm sorry,' she replied, 'but Captain Kumalo is insistent.'

'Since when does the investigating officer decide on this sort of issue? That's your responsibility,' snapped senior counsel. 'Please, let's not waste time here.'

'I'm persuaded by Captain Kumalo, so I'm going to apply for a custodial remand.'

'That's sheer nonsense. You're going to waste the court's time,' barked senior counsel.

As the magistrate entered the courtroom Gary shot a quick glance at the public gallery and observed, with some surprise, Bagley-Smith tucked away in the back row. The magistrate brooked no nonsense from the prosecution, making short shrift of the application for a custodial remand and admonishing the prosecutor for wasting the court's time. He ordered the existing bail conditions to continue except for the daily reporting requirement, and added one additional condition.

'The effect of this order, Mr Winters,' said the magistrate, 'is that you no longer have to report to the police station, but you must at all times remain fitted with your bracelet and within a radius of twenty kilometres of Sandton Police Station. You are to appear in the High Court in Johannesburg two weeks hence at 10 a.m. on 3 February 2020, when a date for trial will be set. Do you understand?'

'Yes, Your Worship.'

'Court is adjourned for fifteen minutes,' said the magistrate.

Relieved that he wasn't to be held in custody, Jeremy's friends and family closed in on him with backslapping, hugging, handshaking and kissing. Gary glanced again to the last row in the public gallery only to see the back of Bagley-Smith's head disappearing through an exit.

Kumalo glared over his shoulder at the defence team as he and Pillay tried to push their way through the noisy, congested courtroom.

Gary ran after them. 'Captain Kumalo, Captain Kumalo,' he yelled. They stopped and waited for him to catch up.

'I hope you're not coming to gloat, Mr Edwards?' said Kumalo, his top lip twitching again.

'I never gloat, Captain, but I do feel immense joy when justice is done. May I collect a copy of your police docket tomorrow? I asked for it five days ago.'

'It'll be ready on Friday. Liaise with Sergeant Pillay.'

'Thank you. I'll call him later.'

On his way back to the rest of the team, a smartly dressed, middle-aged woman intercepted him and extended her right hand. She introduced herself as Ashley Dobson. He recognised the name as the reporter from *The Chronicle*.

'Would you be able to spare me some of your time, whenever it suits you? I plan to do a story on this case and other matters concerning your former firm, and in particular its chairperson.'

'Hello, Ashley,' said Gary with a smile. 'I'll happily meet but only when Jeremy's case is out of the way. I trust you understand. Please excuse me, I need to get back to the others.'

'A quick chat then?'

'You know it would be improper. Please respect that,' said Gary firmly, and at the same time wondering what she was looking into. A story on David Plaistowe?

He pinched a moment with Jeremy and Lucy, both of whom were still grinning. 'Well, just as I promised, Jeremy. You can't let Kumalo get to you. I think he loves playing mind games.'

'I see that now. I'm getting stronger, but still worried about what those two women have told the police.'

Lucy stood by silently, but her beautiful smile said it all. Gary slipped his huge hand over hers and gave it a gentle squeeze, saying, 'That's the spirit, Jeremy, onward and upward as they say. We'll take care of those witnesses when the time is right.'

She snuggled up to Jeremy without saying anything.

'If you're available, Lucy, I'd like to steal you on Saturday to help me work through the police docket,' said Gary, looking first at her and then at Jeremy.

'So, you've got it at last,' said Jeremy. 'Shall I come along?'

'Not yet. Kumalo said I can collect a copy on Friday. Thanks for the offer, but I'd prefer initially to work through all the stuff by myself. I'd like to have Lucy there to help with the usual chronology tables and schedules. Not my strong suit.'

Jeremy frowned and pursed his lips.

'Hey, don't take this the wrong way,' said Gary. 'I can see you're miffed, but I work much better when I haven't got the client looking over my shoulder. Once done, I promise I'll let you have a copy of everything. Are we good?'

'Gary's right. Clients can get in the way and be distracting,' she said, pecking Jeremy on the cheek.

'I guess you're right. I sometimes forget I'm the client.'

Gary cleared the large round table in the study of all its clutter and replaced it with two stacks of documents in preparation for their review of the police docket. Waiting for Lucy to finish a tour of his home, escorted by Charlie, he hooked up his laptop and placed a couple of legal pads, stickers, pens and some highlighters on the table.

'So, what do you think?' he asked when she joined him.

'It's exquisite and so, so fashionably decorated and well kept. And so spacious. A real step up from your last place. This must've cost you a bit.'

He didn't mind her being familiar. They had become close, and as his personal assistant she had become acquainted with most of his personal affairs.

'Thanks, Lucy. I do love the place and, yes, it did cost a bomb by the time the renovators were done, and the interior decorators finished bullying me. At that time I had no one to spend my money on except myself.'

'Not even the swimwear model I've been hearing about?' she asked with a wink.

'Oh, you mean Julia. Nothing serious. We date occasionally. Both of us are far too busy with our careers.'

'That's good to hear. You know, don't you, that you can't get serious with anyone unless and until I approve?'

'Okay, that's enough time wasting,' he said laughingly. 'Here are two copies of the police docket. I'd like us to work through these independently and then compare notes.'

'Anything in particular, you want me to look out for?'

'Keep an open mind and note down anything, no matter how trivial, that catches your attention. Meanwhile make yourself at home. The fridge is fully stocked so help yourself. If you need a break, feel free to go walk-about. In the back garden there's a gate, which leads to Charlie's favourite place, a massive park. I'm sure he would love a little walk if you feel like stretching your legs or getting some fresh air.'

'By the way, have a look at this—found it at my desk after lunch on Friday,' she said.

Gary read the typed note.

As I don't want to risk losing my job, I'm not identifying myself. I thought Gary should know that I was within earshot of Sebastian Bagley-Smith when Jeremy and Amanda left the party. He and James Sanderson were in conversation and I heard him say "She's a delectable little wench. I envy Winters." It was obvious he was referring to Amanda.

He read it a second time before speaking. 'Any idea who might have written this?'

'Not a clue. Maybe you could follow up with James Sanderson,' she suggested.

'No chance there, I'm afraid. He's another one in the chairman's tight circle and big mates with Bagley-Smith. Who knows, this might come in handy down the road.'

He worked methodically through his stack, hoping to find some new evidence to bolster Jeremy's defence. *My goodness, we need it*, he thought to himself. The documents were much as expected: investigation notes and logs written up by Pillay; chain of custody evidence, to avoid suggestions of contamination, in respect of seized crime-scene items and items delivered to laboratories for testing and analysis; numerous photographs and measurements, including those of Amanda's body as she was found by the police, and of Jeremy's car, showing its position in relation to the stairwell and other parking bays; and also of all items taken into custody, such as Amanda's dress, panties, shoes, watch and jewellery, and Jeremy's clothes, shoes and watch. There were also photographs of the scratches on Jeremy's shoulders and chest, and of the ballroom, the elevator lobby area, the front doors of the hotel, various parking basements and the entrance and exit points of the hotel parkade. Finally there were police sketch plans of different locations in and around the hotel with relevant measurements. Gary pushed aside all the documents except for the witness statements. He combed through them slowly, noting down names. Besides Kumalo, Pillay and some other police officers variously involved in the investigation, there were statements from the pathologist, three lab technicians, a fingerprint expert, the security guards who manned the parkade entrance and exit points, the hotel's general manager and its head of security systems and operations, the security guard who discovered the body, David and Roger Plaistowe, Sebastian Bagley-Smith, Jilly and Zara, the couple from the firm's accounts department, and Professor Fundiswa Langa, a psychiatrist attached to one of the teaching hospitals. The last document was a transcript of Jeremy's recorded interview with Kumalo and Pillay.

Gary was surprised that no statement had been taken from Carol Ibbets, the lone woman, given the time of her movement through the fifth basement. Perhaps she hadn't seen or heard anything relevant. *That would be a pity, a great pity.* The absence of mobile phone and car tracking records, and footage from street cameras, served as confirmation of what Pillay had told him about Kumalo's refusal to follow up obvious lines of enquiry.

Keen to know what explanations Bagley-Smith and the Plaistowes had for their seemingly unusual movements after midnight, Gary focused on their statements first.

According to Bagley-Smith he left the party close to 1.30 a.m. with the intention of driving home. He claimed his car wouldn't start because of a flat battery, so he returned to the main foyer via the basement stairs, leaving the hotel through the revolving front door about ten minutes later to catch a taxi home. Strangely, there was no evidence in the docket of him being asked why, given his seniority, he had chosen to park so far down or of any further investigations to check his story.

Roger Plaistowe claimed drunkenness for his vagueness on detail but contended he left the party about half an hour after midnight intending to sleep it off in his car parked in the fifth basement. He didn't deny that he left the elevator at the third basement level but couldn't remember why. He surmised he must have followed others out of the elevator subconsciously. He had no recollection of taking the stairs two flights down to the fifth basement but suggested that would have been the logical thing to do. His explanation for spending forty minutes in the basement area was that he remained in his car trying to sleep. At some point, so he claimed, he felt nauseous and decided to return to the party to see if he could find a lift home instead of using a taxi service.

His explanation for catching the elevator back to the lobby area from the third basement instead of the fifth was that he thought he could get rid of the nausea by walking up the stairs, but that when he arrived at the third basement the nausea had become worse, and that's when he decided to take the elevator.

According to his statement he was relieved to find his father still at the party and asked him for a ride. They took the elevator to the fifth basement so Roger could retrieve his wallet which he claimed he had, through oversight, left in the car. His father then drove him home. He couldn't remember whether they took the stairs or the elevator to get to his father's car.

It became obvious to Gary that father and son had prepared and scripted their statements together. Where there were common areas, the text, in its sequence, format and content, was almost identical. David confirmed that about fifteen to twenty minutes after one o'clock Roger had found him at the party and asked to be taken home. Roger was extremely drunk.

He said that after Roger spent time in the bathroom, they took the elevator to the fifth basement so Roger could retrieve his wallet from his car.

David made a point of emphasising that he and Roger took the stairs from the fifth basement to the ground level parking area where his car was parked. It was at his insistence that they took the stairs because he hoped the exertion would help his son sober up. According to him, after he dropped Roger off at his apartment, he returned to the hotel to search for his mobile phone which he had left in the men's bathroom. He maintained that in his tired state he parked one level too low and had to take the stairs up to the lobby. He claimed that, after retrieving the phone, he returned down the stairs to his car, before heading for home.

Next Gary turned to the statements from the couple from accounts. When read in their entirety, and taking into account their flimsiness, their statements didn't quite paint the picture Kumalo conveyed at the last meeting. They made no comments or observations concerning Jeremy and Amanda's intimacy even before the elevator doors closed, nor did they seek to provide any sort of context for Amanda wanting to return to the party or Jeremy wanting her to accompany him to the car. Nor did they describe how Jeremy supposedly pulled Amanda out of the elevator.

Gary grimaced and occasionally scratched his head as he studied Professor Langa's statement. She was eminently qualified to express an expert opinion on blackouts caused by binge drinking. Although she hadn't interviewed Jeremy, she cast serious doubt on his claim of amnesia. If he had suffered from a blackout, she would have expected him to say so when interviewed by the police, instead of making the statements he made. It was evident that the prosecutor would rely heavily on her opinion to bolster the argument that Jeremy had lied to the police because he knew what he had done.

He pushed back his chair and stood, stretching his arms above his head. 'How about a lunch break, Lucy? I'm famished.'

'Really? You're always famished. You've already put away two ginormous muffins.'

'Listen up, madam, this is a huge machine, needing ample fuel to function,' he replied with a chuckle before rushing around to the other side of the table to pull out her chair with her still seated. She squealed as he carried her and the chair into the kitchen.

'Now you sit there quietly while this chef gets to work.'

In no time at all he produced an inviting salad, sliced some fresh ciabatta bread and laid out an assortment of cheeses.

'I can see you're excited, Lucy, so you go first. What did you discover?'

'A few things in the Bagley-Smith and Plaistowe statements seem peculiar, but there was one thing which jumped out at me,' she replied, shuffling her papers before spreading out photographs of Amanda's dress.

'And what's that?'

'Here, look at these pics. Look carefully.'

He brought the large magnifying glass to one eye and scrutinised the photos closely, first as a group and then individually. 'I'm not seeing anything odd here. What am I missing?'

Standing next to him she delivered a playful slap to his left shoulder. 'Oh, you're hopeless. Have you got a copy of the CCTV footage?'

'I do, but why?'

'Have a close look at Amanda's dress at the party and when she and Jeremy left in the elevator and compare it to the one in the police pics.'

He changed the angle of the screen to avoid the light reflection before rolling the footage, pausing intermittently to make comparisons with the photographs on the table.

Suddenly he jumped up, sending his chair flying and shouted, 'I see it, I see it. This is it.' He grabbed Lucy in a bear hug, lifting her off the floor and danced a little jig.

'Not doubting you, big guy, but tell me what you saw,' she said.

'They're different; the dresses are different. The one in the footage is a halter neck with a low back, the other has thin shoulder straps and a high back.'

'To the top of the class you go,' said Lucy, kissing her index finger before pressing it to his forehead. 'I remember Amanda couldn't decide between the two in the shop, so she bought both. They're identical except for those differences. What does—'

Gary cut in, striding back and forth in his study. 'You know what this means, don't you?'

'I think so,' she replied, grabbing hold of his arm. 'Amanda's dress was changed after she and Jeremy left the party and before she was found in the stairwell. But how and why?'

He stood at the window, rubbing his chin. 'I suppose she could've had the other dress somewhere in the basement and for some bizarre reason decided to change into it.'

'No, no, that's not possible, her other dress was at her home.'

'How do you know?' he asked.

'It came up in conversation near the beginning of the party. She was concerned her dress was too revealing and was toying with the idea of going home to change. Some of the other girls and I persuaded her not to.'

'I don't know how or why, Lucy, but what I do know is that the police have made an almighty blunder here —perhaps even a fatal one. There's nothing in their docket to suggest they searched Amanda's home for other evidence. What happened to the other dress?'

12

For days after discovering the switching of the dresses the temptation to wipe the annoying smugness from Kumalo's face still lingered with Gary. It was only on the advice of the rest of the team that he accepted it would be unwise to confront the police so soon with this new evidence.

He headed to the study and shuffled through a pile of papers until he found what he was after. He scanned his handwritten list of significant points jotted down in random order.

- *Bagley-Smith—movements and lewd comments about Amanda*
- *Plaistowes—movements*
- *Switched dresses*
- *Lone woman in fifth basement*
- *Neck of champagne bottle wiped*
- *Kumalo's reticence to follow potential leads*
- *Kumalo/Plaistowe relationship*

- *Unmonitored stair access to basements*
- *Amanda's physical intimacy towards Jeremy*
- *Flimsiness of statements from accounts department couple*

As he pondered each in turn, and then in conjunction with all the others, his confidence grew exponentially. It might not be necessary after all, he reasoned, to let Jeremy testify in his own defence and risk a damaging cross examination.

Gary paced around the study and out onto the adjacent verandah in search of clarity. Amanda must have changed her dress at some unknown point during the early hours... unless someone else did it for her. Each possibility raised more questions than answers. Whichever way it happened, two pertinent points were abundantly clear: the change occurred after Amanda and Jeremy left the party, and the shoulder-strap dress must have been collected from her home unless Lucy's recollection was wrong. It couldn't be, he figured. That's not something Lucy could have been mistaken about. Besides, some of the other girls could verify that Amanda did not go home to change. If Amanda did the changing, when and by whom was the dress collected, and why did she bother to change after leaving the party to head down to the basement?

Gary returned to the study and reviewed, once again, the CCTV footage to the point where Jeremy and Amanda entered the elevator, all the while keeping his attention on her movements. Before leaving the party with Jeremy, she disappeared from sight periodically, but never long enough to have gone home. It would have taken at least thirty minutes to drive to her cottage, collect the dress and return. So did she perhaps arrange for someone else to go? Although that was a possibility, his gut told him otherwise.

If someone else swapped the dresses, he figured Amanda must have been either unconscious or dead.

But why would someone else have switched the dresses? And how would that person even have known about the other dress and its whereabouts? Needing fresh air and a change of scenery, he called Charlie and they set off for a walk. At any other time, such a diversion would have been peaceful and relaxing, but on this occasion, he came away troubled. Pieces of the puzzle were missing, and he needed to find them.

He wondered about the whereabouts of the other dress and why there were no comments in the police docket about Amanda's missing keys, mobile phone and alarm remote control. Surely these things should have been in her bag found at the scene. Maybe she kept the keys and remote in a secret place at the cottage. He picked up his phone and called Rubin at the Egoli Hotel.

'Hey Rubin, Gary Edwards here. A quick one, if I may? Did any of your staff find a black dress, mobile phone, house keys or an alarm remote control lying around anywhere after our party?'

Somewhat taken aback by the enquiry, Rubin was at a loss for words before he sought context.

'Without boring you with detail,' said Gary, 'it seems these things were misplaced during or after the party, and I'm looking into that for someone.'

Rubin's chuckle revealed his thoughts. 'If that happened, I'm confident I would've been told. Sorry. I hope the lady, or her partner, finds them.' Another chuckle.

Gary began to think about gaining access to Amanda's cottage. Perhaps there might be something there to point the way. Getting in wouldn't be easy. Having lost their only daughter less than two months ago, the last thing her grieving parents would expect or be willing to entertain is an approach from someone representing the accused who had allegedly snuffed out her young life. The media coverage of the rape and murder, and the pointing of the finger at Jeremy, was relentless. Gary had seen how the media hounded anyone associated with the case, including Amanda's parents. They begged to be left alone so they could grieve in private, but their pleas went unheeded.

The delicate nature of the situation couldn't be underestimated. He felt uncomfortable with the idea of a cold call, fearing the reaction of grieving parents. There was also every chance they would alert Kumalo—and that was something he wanted to avoid at all costs. This was not the time to reveal to the police their blunder.

He fleetingly contemplated applying to court for permission to search the house but quickly dismissed the idea. The overwhelming odds were in favour of the judge sending him packing on the grounds that the police should be asked to intervene. After further thought he realised it would be foolhardy to come up with a strategy before finding out what sort of people the Sheltons were.

He phoned Lucy to arrange a meeting for the following afternoon. The intercom buzzer from the security gate cut in on his call. Willem Snyman, the P.I., had arrived exactly on time, as always. Unfortunately he had little to report. Kumalo's lifestyle, as far as Snyman could tell, raised no suspicions. He seemed to live and behave as one would expect of someone earning a captain's salary: no fancy cars or expensive jewellery; an ordinary house in an ordinary neighbourhood; local annual family holidays with inexpensive accommodation; no evidence of lavish entertainment; and no sign of a mistress.

'Is that it?' asked Gary with a furrowed brow. 'A clean cop with a mundane lifestyle who goes on a hunting trip with someone like David Plaistowe?'

'Not quite,' said Snyman. 'Remember, I've only recently started poking around and need more time. I have learned a few things about Kumalo which may interest you. According to some of his former colleagues at his last posting, Kumalo was bitter about having been overlooked for promotion to the rank of inspector, and this has fueled his ambitions in an unhealthy way. That's the first thing. Second, David Plaistowe's fraternisation with Kumalo has gone beyond the one hunting trip.'

'Oh?'

'The two of them visited Mauritius the other day. No family—a midweek trip over two days. My sources tell me they had three or four business meetings at the fanciest hotel on the island.'

'I wonder what that was all about,' said Gary. 'What sort of business could a wealthy, and may I say powerful Johannesburg lawyer and a South African homicide detective be up to in a place like Mauritius?'

'Don't know for sure—does seem unusual though. It doesn't end there. I've been led to believe they're off to Cyprus early next month,' said the P.I.

'To Cyprus? What the hell would they be going to Cyprus for?'

'Take a guess. What's the first thing that comes to mind when you hear about related visits to Mauritius and Cyprus?' asked Snyman.

'Easy and relaxed banking facilities,' said Gary with a snort and a roll of his eyes.

'Exactly. But let's not jump to conclusions. I'll look into this more closely and get back to you.'

Lucy sought out Carol Ibbets at lunchtime, keen to probe more firmly about what she may have seen or heard in the fifth basement. Over the last few weeks, she had managed to establish a closer relationship with Carol who seemed to enjoy her company. They had also met up a couple of times after work for drinks.

She spotted her sitting on her own in the cafeteria. 'Mind if I join you?'

'Of course not. Nice to have your company.'

Lucy led with some small talk, asking her about the time she had spent working in Canada. She said she missed her mother terribly. Her parents were divorced, and her mother decided to remain in Toronto when Carol and her father moved to South Africa about eight months ago.

'How did your father and David Plaistowe become such good friends?' asked Lucy.

'They connected many years back through mining. My dad had, and still has, some mining interests in Canada and here in South Africa; David, who is a mining law specialist, became his personal attorney.'

'How interesting. You must enjoy your work?'

'I do but feel a little awkward at times given the close connection.'

'I guess you have to mind your P's and Q's around the office?'

'I do,' said Carol with a smile. 'My dad wouldn't be pleased if I did anything to embarrass David.'

After a few minutes of inconsequential chatter, Lucy raised the subject matter of Amanda's death. 'Listen, Carol, I want to ask you something about the night of the office party. It's important. There's a lot at stake.'

Carol stiffened noticeably and frowned.

'We won't do anything to embarrass you or compromise you in any way if that's what you're concerned about,' said Lucy.

'What do you want to ask?' enquired Carol in a formal, hesitant tone.

She reminded Carol that she went into the fifth basement shortly before 1 a.m., collected her car and exited the building a few minutes later. 'Did you see or hear anything unusual? Any shouting, screaming, arguing, banging, anything like that?'

Carol paused before replying. 'Why are you asking me this? What makes you think I may have seen or heard something?'

'I don't know if you did, Carol. Somebody raped and murdered that poor girl, and we reckon that could've happened round about the time you left. We're desperate to find the truth and so we're looking at all possible leads.'

Carol fidgeted and chewed on a fingernail. 'Who is "we" and why do you think it wasn't Jeremy? Surely he wouldn't have been sent to the High Court for trial if it weren't him.'

'C'mon Carol, you saw with your own eyes how they were all over each other. Besides, I know Jeremy well and there's no way on earth he could've done this.'

'And the "we"?'

'Jeremy's legal team. I'm helping out where I can because Jeremy's a close friend and my former boss is, as you know, on the defence team.'

'Aren't you afraid? You saw the warning from David.'

'I've no choice. I can't stand by and watch an innocent young guy for whom I care being blamed. I try to be discreet, and if I get caught then so be it, I'll face the consequences.'

Carol leaned forward and glanced from side to side. Lucy waited expectantly. Instead of speaking, Carol sat back, looking up at the ceiling. Lucy waited.

'You're putting me in a terrible predicament,' said Carol. 'My boss has made it clear we're not to talk to anyone about the case except to the police and only when asked by Captain Kumalo. I can't discuss the matter. I'm sorry.'

Gary invited Jeremy to his place so that he and Lucy could brief him on developments. The meeting took a while to get going because Charlie insisted on his share of attention.

'Okay, Charlie, that's enough, we've got some work to do around here.'

Charlie jumped up against Gary's leg, putting on his most imploring look, but when he realised there was no chance, he dragged himself off to his basket.

'I so wish Annie could've had the joy of being with Charlie in his prime,' said Jeremy. 'Oh, how I miss my dear sister.'

'She was special. How different things would have been if Annie was still with us,' said Gary, feeling a wave of guilt.

Having made themselves comfortable on the verandah, Gary enquired of Lucy whether she had told Jeremy about the latest development.

'No, I wanted to wait until the three of us were together. You go ahead, Gary.'

He clasped his hands together and smiled at Jeremy. 'Thanks to Lucy we've made what could be a significant breakthrough.'

He described the switching of the dresses, and elaborated on the timing, the alternative possibilities and the questions it threw up.

Jeremy allowed himself time to digest the latest news before asking, 'And there's nothing in the police docket about this?'

'Not even a hint,' he replied. 'Something's rotten in the State of Denmark or, should I say, the State of Kumalo.'

'I'm astounded, but in a pleasant sort of way. It proves I didn't kill Amanda. As you say, there's something terribly wrong here.'

Gary mentioned Kumalo's apparent refusal to follow up on leads and his relationship with David Plaistowe, at the same time cautioning Jeremy and Lucy to keep these revelations confidential. 'If there's a premature leak it could jeopardise our case which is beginning to look promising.'

He then gave Jeremy an overview of the police docket contents, including the statements made by Jilly and Zara. 'Their statements are thin, Jeremy, extremely thin, and when we have a chance to interview them—if they don't refuse—I suspect Kumalo's accusation that you forced Amanda out of the elevator will lose its fizz.'

'And if they refuse?' asked Jeremy.

'We'll then get the same result at the trial, if there is ever a trial,' said Gary. 'The priority now is to look for the missing dress, and also to get into Amanda's home.'

'Why her home?' asked Jeremy.

'Perhaps the other dress is there,' offered Lucy. 'And there may also be other clues in the cottage.'

'What about the police?' asked Jeremy. 'Have they not already been there?'

'Not according to their docket,' said Gary, 'and if they didn't know about the change of dress, which seems to be the case, there would've been no reason to search. The challenge now is to get access.'

He raised his concerns, especially the reaction Mr and Mrs Shelton were likely to have if he approached them directly.

'Why not ask the court for permission?' suggested Jeremy.

Gary explained why such an approach was risky and undesirable. 'Short of breaking into the place which, on any basis, is a no-no, our only way is to be let in by Amanda's parents. But I don't know them and haven't a clue how best to approach them. Any thoughts, Lucy?'

'It would be a bad idea for you to make the approach. I met them when I went to the cottage with Amanda on the Saturday after we bought our dresses. I also had a brief chat with them at the funeral, and I've visited them and been in touch a few times since then.

Mrs Shelton and I hit it off, but her husband can be quite cranky and difficult.'

'We've got to try,' said Gary. 'Do you think you can give it a go? We've no other choice.'

'I'll have to tread carefully though and work through Mrs Shelton. I'll have to tell her why we want to go into the cottage, which means letting her know about the change of dress.'

'I agree she'll want to know and even more so if we want to take a forensic team in with us,' said Gary. 'That's one helluva risk. I can imagine her telling her husband and he then charging off to Kumalo.'

They spent the rest of the visit working on ways that might lessen the risk of rejection.

Gary walked them out to Lucy's car. 'By the way,' she said, 'I think Carol heard or saw something in that basement and she's too scared to say what.'

'How do you know?' asked Gary.

She told them about their last meeting. 'She wouldn't have said what she said and behaved the way she did if she wasn't withholding something. It wouldn't make sense otherwise.'

'My goodness, how things are suddenly popping up —good things it appears,' said Gary. 'The switching of the dresses, David's questionable relationship with Kumalo, and Carol's odd behaviour. Don't push her any more for the moment. We'll follow up later.'

After the weekend Lucy contacted the Shelton's home. The domestic worker answered the phone. Lucy asked if Mr Shelton was available, ready to cut the call if he was. Luckily, he wasn't so she asked to speak to Mrs Shelton, who soon came on the line.

'Elaine, hi, it's me, Lucy Masters.' After exchanging pleasantries, Lucy reached out tentatively. 'I wonder if we might meet, I've something rather urgent I'd like to talk to you about. It concerns Amanda.'

Lucy could hear a gasp.

'Can't you do it over the phone?' she asked.

'I'm sorry, Elaine, it's too delicate and too sensitive. It really would be better to meet.' She was met with silence. 'Only the two of us. I can't explain now, but you'll understand once we meet.'

A long pause hung uncomfortably in the air. 'If it concerns Amanda shouldn't my husband be there?'

'No,' said Lucy, perhaps too quickly. 'I'll also explain why when we meet. Please, this is terribly important.'

Elaine Shelton finally agreed to meet during Lucy's lunch hour the following day.

'Thank you, I wouldn't be bothering you if this weren't important. And one more thing. Please keep this between the two of us for the moment. Again, you'll understand why when we meet.'

'You're beginning to worry me, Lucy. Is it something bad about my husband?'

'Not at all. It's not like that. I fear that if what I'm going to tell you gets out too soon, even to your husband, it's importance, particularly for your family, might be lost.'

This time the pause was even longer. Lucy waited patiently. 'Okay, I'll see you tomorrow. I liked you from our first meeting; you struck me as a sensible young woman, and I hope you won't disappoint me. I'm sure you can appreciate it's been only seven weeks since Amanda's passing and we're still in an enormous amount of pain.'

The next day Lucy found a discreet spot tucked away in a corner of the salad bar. On time, Elaine Shelton walked through the front door. Lucy caught her eye and beckoned her over. As they hugged, she could feel Elaine trembling.

'Well, here we are. You'll have to forgive me if I'm emotional. It feels like it was only yesterday that our beloved Amanda was so brutally snatched from us.'

Lucy leaned forward across the table, gently placing her hands on top of Elaine's. 'I can't even begin to imagine your grief. I'm so sorry for your suffering and wouldn't have intruded if it weren't important.'

Elaine turned her eyes to the ceiling, wiping at them with her fingers, trying to avoid smudging her mascara. They placed their orders but when the food came Elaine scratched around unenthusiastically before pushing her plate away. She sipped at her coffee and waited silently.

Although tempted to check that Elaine hadn't mentioned the meeting to her husband, Lucy restrained herself.

'Thank you for meeting with me,' she said. 'I know this is a tough time and you probably don't want to hear anything about the police investigation, but we think the police have messed up badly.'

Elaine cut in. 'Who is "we"?'

'Gary Edwards and me.'

'Is he not on the team defending that pervert who killed our daughter?' she asked, scowling. 'And where do you fit into all this?'

Lucy had to keep her wits about her. *This can so easily go wrong*, she thought.

'You're right, he's on the defence team and I'm helping out because I used to work for him.'

Elaine stood and snatched her bag off the table. 'How dare you play with our feelings?' she hissed. 'I thought you were better than that.'

Lucy quickly grabbed Elaine by the wrist. 'Please, Elaine, I'm going out on a limb here, but know you'll understand once you hear what I've got to say. Please, please, it's important.'

Elaine jerked her arm free and took her seat, glaring across the table.

'Thank you,' whispered Lucy. 'I have with me a video clip from the hotel's CCTV footage from that awful night, which shows Amanda wearing a halter neck dress when she left the party with Jeremy Winters. You're welcome to watch if you want to, but first I want to show you photos taken by the police of the dress she was wearing when they found her.' She slid across the police photos. 'If you look closely, you'll see a dress with shoulder straps.'

Elaine took her time looking at each photograph and then scrutinised them again, and again.

'May I see the video clip now?' she asked.

'Are you sure, Elaine? Both Amanda and Jeremy had too much to drink.'

'Let me see.'

Lucy ran the clip showing them leaving the ballroom, up until they entered the elevator. She knew it would be painful for Elaine to see her daughter behaving that way but wanted her to be aware of the intimacy between the two of them. Elaine watched the clip four times before she closed the laptop and pushed it across the table. Tears streamed down her cheeks as she ferreted in her handbag for tissues.

Lucy moved in next to her, placing her arm across Elaine's shoulders. Elaine leaned in, dropping her head onto Lucy's chest. After a while she sat back, wiping at her moist cheeks. 'What does this mean?' she asked, still sniffing.

Lucy returned to her side of the table. 'Obviously someone switched the dresses.'

'Who?' asked Elaine.

'We're not sure yet. I guess it's possible Amanda snuck home after she and Jeremy left the party and then returned to the hotel after changing. But why? It doesn't make sense. One thing's for certain, there's something wrong here and we intend to find out. We need your help, Elaine.'

'How?'

'We need to find the halter neck dress so we can have it forensically examined for clues. Would you allow us to look around the cottage?'

Elaine hesitated, transferring her weight onto her elbows and covering her face with her hands. Lucy beckoned the waiter and asked for a glass of water.

'I'll have to discuss this with my husband,' said Elaine. 'We've not been into the cottage. It's the way it was when Amanda left for the party. We haven't been able to go in there.'

Lucy again took hold of Elaine's trembling hands and held them firmly. 'Elaine,' she said in a hushed tone, 'I understand, but we need to get a forensic team in there to search for clues that might help in bringing closure and indeed, justice.'

'Let me talk to my husband and get back to you.'

'Please, I beg of you, keep this between us. It's not that we have any suspicions against your husband, it's that he may want to confront the police, and that's something we want to avoid at this point, given what we know. At best, they've blundered. It's even possible there's some sort of cover-up going on.'

'What cover-up?' she asked in a clipped tone, sitting upright.

'I can't talk about that now because certain enquiries are being followed up. As soon as I know more, I'll let you know.'

Elaine rested her elbows on the table again and placed her chin on interlocked hands. Her eyes flicked from side to side and then focused on Lucy. 'I need to think on this.'

13

Convinced the missing dress would be the key to finally identifying Amanda's attacker, and suspicious of Kumalo's odd behaviour, Gary came up with a decoy strategy to shield, at least for the time being, what he and the team knew about the switching of the dresses. He would give Kumalo and the prosecutor the false impression that the defence was heavily focused on the dress depicted in the police photographs.

He contacted the prosecutor to let him know that he intended to meet with Kumalo to arrange for the defence team and its appointed experts to have access to the dress in their custody.

'Why?' asked the prosecutor.

'We want our own experts to analyse the dress for trace evidence. We think the dress is going to be pivotal in determining the outcome of the case,' said Gary.

'Really?' queried the prosecutor, surprised. 'Am I missing something here?'

'Well, according to your expert witness, no trace evidence was found on the dress. We've every reason to believe that's nonsense, so we want our own experts to have a look.'

By the time Gary called Kumalo an hour later, the prosecutor had already been in touch with him.

'The prosecutor tells me you clever lawyers think we've cocked up the forensics on the dress,' said Kumalo. 'My, my, I wish we were as clever as you guys. So, you think you're going to find something on the dress which shows someone else did this?'

'We do, Captain Kumalo. We definitely do. We've got reason to think so.'

'And why do you think that?' asked Kumalo.

'Like you, I'm not in the business of sharing case information unless the law compels me to, so I'm afraid you're going to have to wait for the big reveal in due course,' replied Gary, struggling to stifle his laughter.

A prolonged silence followed before Kumalo said a meeting was unnecessary. He told Gary to contact Detective Sergeant Pillay for the handover.

Gary's phone call to Pillay the following day confirmed the effectiveness of the strategy. Kumalo had apparently informed Pillay that the dress had become a 'material and most significant factor' in the case and that Pillay had better, under threat of severe consequences, have the dress examined by a different expert.

With chain of custody evidence carefully and properly taken care of, the dress was handed over to the laboratory technicians appointed by the defence team. Gary exaggerated to Pillay how long it could be before the defence experts were done. 'We might also bring out to South Africa a renowned expert from Scotland to assist in the tests and analysis,' said Gary.

'You're not serious?' asked Pillay.

'Given what we've discovered, you bet we are,' said Gary, rather pleased with himself.

At last, time for a bit of rest and recreation. Gary looked forward to a break with Julia. They both needed time away, she from her punishing modelling assignments, mostly abroad, and he from Jeremy's case and his own family matters. He seemed to have been involved in nothing else for weeks on end. It was time to kickback and recuperate. He knew Julia felt the same way.

On their first morning in the Drakensberg, they set out after breakfast on an unguided hike from Cathedral Peak Hotel to Ribbon Falls. The trail led them through breathtaking views of green valleys and towering peaks. As soon as the path widened, Julia drew alongside him, taking his hand as they continued the gentle climb. 'You're not relaxing, Gary—want to talk about it?'

'I'm sorry, it's a bit tough going at the moment, worrying about Jeremy's case, my commitments with no income, and about my family. My mum's a wreck, watching my father die.' He squeezed her hand. 'Thank you for asking, hopefully it won't be too long before my life's back to normal.'

She stopped and folded her arms around his neck. 'I care about you, dearest Gary, our relationship means a great deal to me—*you* mean a great deal to me—and I feel terribly sad seeing you like this.'

He hugged her back. 'Thank you, Julia, thank you, that means a lot to me. I also care about you, but I'm afraid with the way things are going I'm not going to be able to maintain my lifestyle much longer.'

She stepped back and slapped him softly on the shoulder. 'Gary Edwards! Do you really think your lifestyle is important to our relationship? It's you I love... I mean, like, and not your material trappings.

Please understand that.' Again, she hugged him, and after pausing, said, 'No, I didn't get it wrong—I do love you. It's early days, I know, but I've never felt like this about any other man.'

'I don't know what to say, Jules. I confess I've always thought you saw me as a good friend with whom you have a comfortable, casual, relationship, and that the busyness of your career ruled out anything more.'

She waited for him to say more but he remained silent, settling himself on a large rock. She sat cross-legged in front of him, taking a few sips from her water bottle. 'And now that I've told you otherwise, what do think?' she asked.

'I'm overcome—I'm flattered—I too have feelings for you. I've only been in love once before, and that was some years back.'

The little voice inside him whispered that he should share his love for her, but he was reticent, unsure whether he was ready for commitment. She frowned as he helped her back on her feet. They continued walking, climbing higher towards the falls, preoccupied with their own thoughts. Fifteen minutes later Julia again took his hand.

'People tend to categorise models, particularly successful ones, as rich super bitches who care only about themselves, money and fleeting relationships,' she said. 'I'm not like that, Gary. Yes, I make a lot of money and I'm financially independent, but I care about things that matter—love, loyalty, friendships, family, home, pets like Charlie, and so on, and so on.'

'I know, I've never doubted you,' he replied. 'In many ways, we are similar and that's why we have something special. Now, let's get up to that waterfall before we change our minds.'

Time flew by and before they knew it they were packing up on their last morning together to return home.

'Well, I guess all good things come to end,' said Julia.

He took her hands and looked into her mesmerising green eyes. 'That was a brilliant time. I'm sad we couldn't have stayed longer. I hope you're now convinced you're not my last resort go-to girl,' he said with an impish smile.

Her soft hands enveloped his cheeks as she moved in, close to him, and then kissed him passionately. 'I'm convinced, and hope you know I'm here for you.'

'Thank you, I do.'

He hadn't been home long before his phone buzzed. He could hear the excitement in Lucy's voice as she blurted out her news. Elaine Shelton had agreed to allow them to examine Amanda's home. 'And she's promised not to tell her husband. He'll be out of town next week so that will be a good time.'

'Well done, Lucy, you're truly a miracle worker. I think this could well be another eureka moment,' he said.

'Let me know ASAP when suits you. I don't want to lose momentum with Elaine.'

'I'll call you within the hour.'

'By the way, I'm meeting Carol for drinks after work. She invited me. Hold thumbs.'

'You're on a roll, aren't you? Push hard if you have to. If need be, tell her we'll subpoena her at the trial where she'll have to answer questions under oath.'

'Okay. Before you go, aren't you forgetting something?' asked Lucy.

'What?'

'You haven't told me how your weekend was with your sexy model.'

'Restful and peaceful and deeply meaningful.'

'Peaceful and meaningful, maybe, but restful—naaaaagh,' she said, and terminated the call.

She found Carol, drink in hand, sitting alone at a table in the beer garden where they agreed to meet.

'Hey, Carol, that looks good. I'm going to have the same,' she said beckoning the waiter and at the same time donning sunglasses to shield her eyes against the setting sun. Carol ordered another beer for herself.

As before, they kicked off with small talk and then Carol suddenly became serious. 'I haven't been open with you on the question you asked me.'

She paused. Lucy didn't interrupt.

'I'm scared. You don't know my dad. He can be aggressive, I mean physically aggressive, and I don't want to cross him.'

'But how will you be crossing him?'

'I've told you he and David are close friends and I only got employed because of their friendship.'

'I don't understand,' said Lucy, feigning ignorance.

'If it gets back to David that I've been talking to you about the case he'll explode and tell my dad, then all hell will break loose.'

'Whatever you tell me will, I repeat, will be kept in the strictest confidence.'

'You won't even bring it up in the trial or with anyone else for that matter?' Carol queried.

'I promise. I'm intrigued, though, why did you want to meet if you're so worried?'

'It's bothering me terribly that the police might have the wrong person. I've been struggling to sleep since the party because I've kept quiet. I don't want to see an innocent man go down for the murder of Amanda.'

Lucy couldn't contain herself. 'Are you saying you saw what happened?'

'No, I didn't, but I heard something.'

'What?' said Lucy, moving closer.

Carol called the waiter and ordered another round of beers and two shots of tequila.

'When I got out of the elevator in the basement, I heard a helluva commotion coming from the direction of the stairwell. A man and a woman were arguing and shouting. I heard the woman say "Get away from me, get away, I'm not interested" or something like that. He screamed back at her, something along the lines of "You've just fucked him in his car. Am I not good enough for you? Is that it? Answer me, is that it, you bloody whore?" Again she shouted, telling him to leave her alone. It sounded like a drunken quarrel. I didn't want to get dragged into it, so I hurried off to my car.'

Lucy sat back, not having expected anything like this. She slugged back her shot and chased it with the beer.

'Are you sure? What you've told me could be exactly what saves an innocent young man being sent to prison for life. But more than that, it will mean closure for Amanda's parents.'

'I am, and I know. Can I get you another?' she asked, calling over the waiter.

'Not for me, I've got to drive,' said Lucy.

'Well, it's Uber for me,' said Carol, ordering another for herself.

Lucy was keen not to interrupt Carol's flow. 'Did you recognise the voices?'

Carol hung her head on her chest, wincing, and then she stood, saying she needed a pee, before wandering off in the general direction of the toilets. Lucy watched her unsteady gait, not sure what to make of the astounding revelation. She was also not sure whether Carol would be returning.

Twenty minutes later, thinking Carol had gone, Lucy caught a glimpse of her across the garden, steadily pushing her way through the crowd in Lucy's direction, mobile to her ear. Carol sat down and leant in close. 'You asked me if I recognised the voices,' she said, speaking slowly and deliberately, trying to disguise the slur.

Lucy held her breath in anticipation. 'I didn't know Amanda so can't tell whether it was her voice I heard. Because of what happened I assume it was her.'

Another long pause. Lucy felt like shaking her but knew that wouldn't help. 'The man's voice sounded a bit familiar,' whispered Carol, 'but I can't be sure.'

Dammit, thought Lucy.

'But who did it sound like?' asked Lucy.

'I can't, I simply can't, it's not right,' she replied.

'Could you tell whether it was a young man's voice or an older person's voice? Any accent or nuances?'

'Not sure. It sounded a bit posh. You know how some people at the office speak,' she said. Carol dropped her head into her palms and sat quietly.

'Come, I'll give you a lift home,' said Lucy, taking her arm as they wended their way to the car.

Lucy called Gary as soon as she arrived home and shared the revelation of another man arguing with Amanda.

'I think Carol either knows or has a strong suspicion who the guy was. She's frightened. I suspect she decided to clam up because she had already said too much.'

'My word. The bit she's told you will be enough to exonerate Jeremy but only if she's willing to make an official statement.'

'Forget it, I gave her my word that we'll keep this confidential.'

14

Elaine Shelton waved tentatively as the two cars eased their way up the driveway of the cottage shielded from the road and neighbours by the overgrown garden. The main house stood an appreciable distance away, separated from the cottage by a row of mature oak trees along their common boundary.

Lucy, on a day's leave, took care of the introductions.

'Thank you, Mrs Shelton,' said Gary. 'I know this is painfully difficult for you, but we know enough to believe our intrusion won't be in vain.'

'Elaine, please call me Elaine,' she said in a cracking voice, wiping at her eyes with the back of her hand.

An awkward silence followed. 'If you want to go inside would you mind slipping these on?' Gary said, holding out some crime scene gear. The others were already pulling theirs on.

'No, I can't. I can't,' she stammered, her eyes welling up and taking a few steps back. 'As I told Lucy, we've not been able to go in there since Amanda's passing.'

'I understand,' he said, donning the last piece of protective equipment.

Elaine keyed the Yale lock on the front door and invited them to go in. 'Please pull the door shut when you're done and give me a call,' she said.

Although Jeremy knew of the visit, Gary hadn't invited him to join them, mainly because he wanted to avoid too many people traipsing through the cottage. He and Lucy were fully up to speed on the protocols to be followed and, if in any doubt, they had been told to check with one of the technicians. They could observe and look around, but under no circumstances were they to touch anything. If they wanted anything examined or noted they had to ask.

The distinct musty smell of stale air confirmed the cottage had been closed up for the two months since Amanda's death. A few things struck Gary as soon as he walked through the front door: a set of keys, including a Yale key and an alarm remote control, hung from a key rack on the wall; the pot plants were shrivelled; the blinds and curtains were drawn closed; and a small, crumpled rug and a white dressing gown lay on the carpeted floor in the passageway that led to the bedroom. Eerily, a TV music channel, turned down low, played classical music.

They followed the technicians on their initial sweep. One photographed whilst the other dictated observations into a voice recorder. The double bed, although made up, appeared to have been lain on at the side nearest the door. Gary noticed a mobile phone on the bedside table. A coat hanger embossed with the logo of the boutique where Amanda and Lucy had shopped for the dress lay on the floor at the base of the open closet doors. Another similar hanger hung in the closet. A large bath towel hung over the shower door. Gary moved cautiously to the closed waste bin in the corner and called over one of the technicians, asking him to check inside.

'There's something in here,' said the technician. 'Let us take some photographs first.'

They stood to one side, allowing the necessary photographs to be taken outside as well as inside the bin, and of its position in the bathroom. When the technician was done, he retrieved what he had seen earlier and held it up in his gloved hand. Both Gary and Lucy gasped loudly; she brought her cupped hands to her mouth, and he punched the air, not once, but twice, saying almost breathlessly, 'Yes, yes, dammit yes!' Then they embraced, slapping each other on the back. 'That's it, that's the missing dress,' responded Lucy.

'No doubt,' said Gary. 'That's our jackpot. I knew it, dammit, I knew it.'

The technician bagged the dress, smiling at the two of them.

Gary and Lucy were decidedly happy to remove themselves from the cottage so the technicians could get on with the rest of the forensics.

'How long do you guys expect to be?' asked Gary.

'Between two to three hours,' replied a white-suited figure. 'We'll give you a call when we're almost done.'

Gary and Lucy drove towards Emmarentia Dam to kill time and get some fresh air.

'So, what do you think?' asked Lucy.

'Without a doubt Amanda came home that night. Her front door key and alarm remote control are hanging on the key rack, the halter neck dress is disposed of in the waste bin, her mobile phone is on the bedside table, and her gown is thrown on the floor.'

'It sure looks that way,' agreed Lucy.

'There aren't any signs of forced entry or a struggle.'

'Suggesting what?'

'We know Amanda ended up back at the hotel,' said Gary. 'Either she returned voluntarily or someone took her back against her will. If she was forced, I'd expect to see some signs of a struggle, but there aren't any.'

'Isn't it possible that she *was* forced, but by someone she knew well enough to let into her home? That might also explain why there was no struggle. I can't get my head round her coming home so late, changing, and then going back to the hotel basement. Why?'

'I hear you. None of it makes sense. Why would someone force her to go back to the basement?'

He left his question hanging in the air as they parked next to the public rose garden. They ambled through the garden, pausing often to smell or admire some of the roses.

'If, and this is a big if, Amanda was overpowered in her home and taken back to the hotel basement, here's how and why it could've happened.' She listened intently as he unpacked his theory. When he was done, she suggested they walk around the dam.

'I don't know what to say,' she said. 'It sounds bizarre, yet, in an odd sort of way, quite logical.' She pondered for a moment before asking, 'Where to from here?'

'I need to figure that out. We know Amanda came home and we know her body ended up back at the hotel. The in-between stuff is murky, but still not that bad for us.'

'I don't understand.'

'Do we now have enough for the police to drop the charges?' he said.

He saw the look on her face and jumped in before she could reply. 'I know, I know, that's not good enough. We must find the killer to rid Jeremy of the dark cloud hanging over him.'

'Precisely. It's going to be interesting to see what the forensics come up with.'

'I can't wait.'

On the way back to the cottage Gary asked Lucy to approach Carol for a meeting with him. 'If she can identify the male voice from the stairwell, that will be game, set and match,' he said with hope.

'I think it might be better to ambush her. She enjoys a drink, so why don't I invite her out after work, and you just happen to walk in on us?'

'Great idea. Let me know when. Meanwhile I'll have a closer look at the CCTV footage that covers the hotel entrance. We know Amanda didn't leave through the parkade exit, and if she came back on her own, she would've entered through the front doors.'

'Shouldn't we also check with the taxi companies?' asked Lucy. 'She must've taken a taxi home and possibly back again.'

'Good call. Can I leave that with you?'

'Of course, I'll get onto it.'

On their arrival the forensics team was just about done. 'Anything worth mentioning?' enquired Gary.

'We managed to lift lots of fingerprints from the countertop near the kitchen sink, the shower door handle, the bathroom taps, a drinking glass in the kitchen sink, and the front door handle. They were from different people. Could be old prints from family or friends. We also took samples of the carpet fibres. But these won't mean much unless we have something to compare them to.'

'Understood,' said Gary. 'Who knows, as the investigation progresses a comparison might become possible.'

A few minutes later, as the technicians drove off, Elaine Shelton emerged along a narrow path in the garden. She looked first at Gary and then at Lucy before returning her attention to him. 'Did you find what you were looking for?'

'We did, thank you,' he said, and then told her about the halter neck dress and other noticeable evidence, summarising the findings of the forensic team.

'She closed her eyes and brought her hands to her face. Her body shook as she wept. Lucy stepped up quickly to comfort her, asking whether there was somewhere they could sit.

Gary pulled the front door closed. When he turned around Lucy was steering Elaine down the footpath along which she had come. He followed them to the Sheltons' house.

'Won't you put the kettle on for some tea?' asked Elaine, drawing deep, sniffing breaths and at the same time pointing Gary towards the kitchen. She and Lucy made their way to the lounge where he joined them after a few minutes with the tea.

'I can't understand how and why our Amanda ended up back at the hotel, in the basement,' said Elaine.

'We're grappling with the same questions, and others,' he said. 'We will find answers, however long it takes.'

He raised the alternative possibilities, emphasising the fact that there were no signs of a forced entry.

'What does that mean?' asked Elaine, again sniffing.

'If Amanda was attacked in the cottage, it must've been by someone she let in, meaning she knew him or her.'

'What happens now and what does all this tell you? I wish my husband were here,' she said, beginning to cry again, quietly into her hands. Again, Lucy comforted her.

He waited until she stopped crying. She leaned back on the sofa, dabbing at her eyes, and looked at him for an answer.

'A few things,' he said. 'We now know for certain that Amanda came back to the cottage after having been with Jeremy Winters and, because we know he never left the hotel before his arrest, we can be sure he had nothing to do with the attack. We also know Amanda ended up back at the hotel in a different dress. We don't know why or how. We also know the police have bungled and not followed some obvious leads.'

'Such as?'

'Elaine, what I'm about to share with you is sensitive and, I might add, crucial to our ongoing investigations. You can't tell anyone, I mean anyone, or about our visit here today, because if the police or the Plaistowes find out where we're heading, the truth may never come out. Can we count on you?'

'I hate keeping things from my husband. We've no secrets, but I understand. You can count on me.'

He then told her about Kumalo and David Plaistowe having what seemed like an inappropriate relationship, and about Kumalo's failure to follow clear lines of enquiry.

There was only so much Elaine Shelton could take for one day, so Gary and Lucy decided to call it a day. She walked them to his car.

'We'll now wait for our forensic chaps to run all their tests and we'll be following up on some other things. We'll update you as soon as we have anything worthwhile to feed back.'

Elaine pushed the passenger door shut with a parting shot. 'Find the bastard who did this to our little girl.'

15

Gary had hoped that by now the leader of the defence team, Advocate Herbert Dlamini, would have persuaded Bagley-Smith and the Plaistowes to make themselves available for an interview, together with some of the other prosecution witnesses. The prosecutor had no objection, confident no harm could be done, so certain was he in his case. David Plaistowe, on the other hand, would have none of it, and the other two, not unexpectedly, simply followed his lead. He expressed his disappointment that someone of Dlamini's stature would not accept the statements to the police at face value.

Dlamini returned a missed call from Gary.

'Thanks for calling back, Herbert. Any further thoughts on getting Bagley-Smith and the Plaistowes to agree to an interview?'

'It's a difficult one. David Plaistowe is quite clearly speaking for all of them. He is, as you know, extremely arrogant and gets quite tetchy at the slightest hint of anyone doubting his word. I suggested to him that perhaps he should take legal advice on the potential risk of refusing to be interviewed. He exploded, reminding me of his standing and credentials, saying he was fully acquainted with the law and not in need of advice either from myself or anyone else.'

'How about switching tack?' asked Gary.

'What do you have in mind?'

'How about telling him you're thinking about the possibility of advising Jeremy to offer a plea bargain to the prosecutor, but that you wouldn't feel comfortable doing that unless you could first interview the three of them and come away satisfied with the answers they give?'

'You mean hold out the possibility of the case being finalised quickly and so ridding his firm of the ongoing bad publicity?'

'Precisely, David's ego will, I bet, drive him to jump at the suggestion.'

Advocate Dlamini pondered on this for a few moments. 'I like it. David might not believe me though, given that I didn't mention this when I approached him last time. Leave it with me.'

Three days later, Dlamini reverted with the news that the interviews were on.

'Did he query why your previous approach was different?' asked Gary.

'Oh, very much so. I told him I was reticent about sharing the possibility of a guilty plea but that having reflected on the matter and with regard to his good reputation I believed he would keep the disclosure to himself. That did the trick, and he was happy for the interviews to take place in the boardroom of my chambers next week on Thursday and, if need be, Friday.'

Given his hostile departure from the firm and the attitude of the managing partners about his involvement in Jeremy's defence preparation, Gary decided not to attend.

Bagley-Smith was first up. He sat across from Dlamini at the polished boardroom table, empty, save for a small bottle of water and two clean glasses, placed there by the advocate. After thanking Bagley-Smith for his attendance and introducing him to the stenographer and other members of the team, he began his questioning.

'I believe Amanda Shelton was a paralegal in your department, the tax department. Is that correct?'

'Yes.'

'Were you and are you still the head of that department?'

'Indeed, I am.'

'My understanding is that it's the most successful department in the firm in terms of fee generation and profitability. Is that correct?'

'Yes, by a wide margin, I have to say.'

'Is it also correct that your department handles a considerable amount of offshore work involving, amongst others, the Caymans and the jurisdictions of Mauritius and Cyprus?'

'Yes,' replied Bagley-Smith with a frown.

Although the defence team had nothing on him concerning those dealings, they had decided to mention those places, knowing he would tell Plaistowe. If there was anything untoward going on between him and Kumalo this might cause a bit of consternation.

'Are you and have you always been a caring boss?'

'Of course.'

'I've been told your department is highly respected by many, including amongst offshore corporates. Is that so?'

'I like to think so,' he said, sitting tall and rubbing the palms of his hands together.

'And that, because of your able leadership, it enjoys an enviable reputation in the broader tax community?'

'We try our best,' said Bagley-Smith, sitting even taller.

Advocate Dlamini continued in the same vein, setting Bagley-Smith at ease, and painting him as the consummate professional and boss. Then he began to home in on what mattered.

'What sort of employee was Amanda?'

'Excellent. She was highly competent, efficient and reliable. I trained her myself.'

'That's most commendable. And what sort of person was Amanda in terms of her personality and attitude to life?'

'She was friendly, gregarious and unselfish. She could be feisty when provoked, but altogether a lovely, decent young woman who upheld the high standards of the firm.'

'Did you ever work late hours with Amanda?'

'Yes.'

'And how did she get home on those occasions?'

'Either I drove her home, or I arranged for one of the other men in my department to drive her.'

'To her cottage in Rivonia?'

'Yes.'

'And how would she get to work the following day?'

'She either took an Uber or another taxi service and the firm reimbursed her. I'm a little lost, why are you asking these questions?' queried Bagley-Smith. He unscrewed the bottle of water and filled his glass.

'Purely for background purposes, nothing to worry about,' said Dlamini before continuing with his questions.

'On the night of the party did you see any interaction between Jeremy Winters and Amanda?'

He brought a fist to his mouth and coughed into it. 'Who didn't, given the way they carried on.'

Bagley-Smith raised the glass to his lips and took a deep draught.

'Enlighten me,' said Dlamini.

'Well, they were drunk, extremely drunk and slobbering all over each other on the dance floor.'

'Please be more specific.'

'They clung on, kissed often, with Amanda's provocatively short dress creeping up more than a few times, leaving little to the imagination.'

'Did this cause embarrassment?' asked Dlamini.

'It certainly did, not only for me, but also for many others, including senior partners.'

'I presume you or one of the other senior partners had a word with them?'

Bagley-Smith coughed and spluttered and then scratched above his right ear, dislodging white specks of dandruff.

'Well did you or did you not?' asked Dlamini.

'No, it wasn't my place to admonish another partner, even one junior to me.'

'But you are one of the managing partners, are you not?'

'I am.'

Dlamini shifted up a gear. 'Did you see them leave the party?'

'Yes, hanging onto each other and, if I remember correctly, Winters had a bottle of champagne with him.'

'What did you think was going to happen?'

'If they didn't pass out, it was pretty obvious.'

'I take it they appeared as keen as each other?'

'Certainly seemed so.'

'James Sanderson is one of the partners in your department, is he not?' asked Dlamini.

'Yes,' said Bagley-Smith, shuffling in his chair and again scratching above his right ear.

'Did you have any alcohol to drink at the party?'

'Yes, but a modest amount, not enough to affect my faculties,' he said, exaggerating his affected English accent.

'Do you remember being in conversation with James at the time that Amanda and Jeremy left the party?'

Bagley-Smith looked down and blinked nervously. 'Do you mind if we have a bathroom break for ten minutes?' he asked, again shuffling in his chair.

'Let's finish this point, and then of course. I don't want to lose my train of thought,' said Dlamini.

'I have no independent recollection, but it's possible,' came the response.

'Well let me help you,' said Dlamini, making a show of holding up a piece of paper and reading from it. 'Did you not say to Sanderson, as Jeremy and Amanda left, "She's a delectable little wench. I envy Winters"?'

Bagley-Smith's face reddened as he jumped up, 'This is preposterous,' he shouted, 'what the hell are you trying to do?' He grabbed his jacket and headed for the door.

Dlamini called after him, 'We'll wait for you for ten minutes.'

Before the ten minutes were up, he returned, grumbling, and pocketing his mobile phone.

'Who've you been calling, Mr Bagley-Smith?'

'That's irrelevant to this interview,' he snapped. He picked up the glass of water and took a mouthful.

'Well, if this case ever goes to trial, I'll ask you then and I'm quite sure the judge will compel you to answer. Let's move on. Is it not usual at functions, like your firm's parties, for the managing partners to enjoy reserved parking close to the main entrance?'

'I don't know what you're driving at,' said Bagley-Smith, now striking a defiant and obnoxious demeanour.

'I've noticed a sudden aggressive attitude on your part, Mr Bagley-Smith. What is the reason for that?'

The interviewee glared again before replying. 'The reason is quite simple, Advocate Dlamini. Your innuendos are offensive and I won't put up with it.'

'Let me try again,' said Dlamini firmly. 'My understanding is that the managing partners enjoy certain perks, one of them being preferential parking at firm functions held away from the office. Is that correct?'

'Sometimes, yes,' said Bagley-Smith, this time scratching above both ears, dislodging more dandruff.

'Let's get specific. I've been informed that all the managing partners had reserved parking at the ground level entrance of the Egoli Hotel at the time of the party. Is that where you parked, and if not, where did you park?'

'This is becoming insulting,' he shouted. 'I refuse to play your little game. Enough is enough.' He stood up, ready to leave.

'You can storm out if you like, Mr Bagley-Smith, but eventually you'll have to answer my questions, even if it's at the trial when you're under oath to tell the truth.'

The two locked eyes, neither saying a word. Eventually Bagley-Smith backed down, returning to his chair, and wiping his brow with a lace handkerchief.

Dlamini took this as an invitation to continue with his questions. 'Where did you park?'

'In the fifth basement.'

'Why there?'

He hesitated before answering. 'I don't know. It was probably a subconscious thing. I really can't tell now.'

'The hotel's CCTV footage shows you taking the elevator down to the fifth basement at one twenty-five on the Sunday morning and that's the last we see of you. There's no evidence of you leaving by car or returning to the main lobby. What happened to you?'

Bagley-Smith repeated what he had told the police: his vehicle wouldn't start, so he returned to the lobby via the stairs, left the hotel through the front doors and took a taxi home.

'Why didn't you take the elevator back to the lobby?'

'I'm not sure.'

'At what time did you return to the lobby and head out of the front door?'

'I wasn't in the basement long, so my best estimate is that I left the hotel at about one thirty-five.'

'Do you remember the name of the taxi company?'

'No.'

'How did you pay?'

'Cash.'

On further questioning, Bagley-Smith said he didn't hear or see evidence of an argument or assault in the fifth basement and if there had been a body in the stairwell between the fifth and sixth basements, he would not have been aware of it. He also said that his taxi ride wouldn't have taken him towards Rivonia because he lived in Dunkeld, in the opposite direction.

'We're nearly done,' said Dlamini. 'Are you agreeable to your mobile phone service provider making available to us data showing the movements of your mobile phone from 1.25 a.m. to four o'clock on the Sunday morning?'

'Definitely not. That would be a gross violation of my right to privacy.'

'Finally, do you deny you said to Sanderson, that Amanda was a delectable little wench and you envied Jeremy? Think carefully, Mr Bagley-Smith, before you answer.'

'Look, you know what it's like... end of a tough year, lots of banter, some drinks, occasional locker room talk amongst the boys. I guess I may have said that jokingly.'

'I see, and thank you for your time,' said Dlamini.

Dlamini waited for him to leave the room before putting on a pair of latex gloves and bagging Bagley-Smith's glass.

16

An hour later, before the interview with his son, David Plaistowe called the advocate for the defence.

'Good day, Mr Dlamini, I believe you gave Bagley-Smith a rough time. That's not what I understood would happen when I agreed to the interviews.'

'Mr Plaistowe, I told you I was considering advising my client to offer a plea bargain provided I was satisfied with the outcome of the interviews. This means I must robustly examine what each of you have said to the police, otherwise how can I in good conscience make any sort of judgment concerning Jeremy's guilt. That's why I was at times firm with Bagley-Smith and why I'm bound to be firm with your son and, perhaps, even with you.'

'I know it was harrowing for poor Bagley-Smith, and could be for my son, so go easy man. I'm not concerned for myself, so knock yourself out when it comes to me. I'm keen to get this damn embarrassment out of the way soon, it's costing my firm in more ways than you could ever imagine.'

'I appreciate your understanding, Mr Plaistowe. See you later.'

Roger Plaistowe strutted past Advocate Dlamini's secretary and shoved open the boardroom door. Dispensing with the usual greetings, he announced, 'I'm here for my interview. Let's get on with it, shall we. I've another appointment in an hour.'

Seeing the incredulous look on the faces of the stenographer and his legal team, Dlamini felt his hackles rise. He was sorely tempted to tear a strip off the arrogant young man, but resisted, not wanting to risk him storming off.

'Thank you for meeting with us. I'm sure we'll be done long before your next appointment.'

Plaistowe had brought a bottle of water, which he slammed down on the boardroom table before slouching back in the chair.

'Here's a glass and some more water in case of need,' said Dlamini.

Plaistowe ignored the courtesy.

'Where do you live?' asked Dlamini.

'In an apartment at Melrose Arch,' he replied, puffing out his chest. His glance skipped to everyone in the room, looking for acknowledgement of the exclusivity of the neighbourhood.

'Were you living there at the time of your firm's party in early December?'

'Yes, I've lived there for a few years.'

'To get to your apartment from the Egoli Hotel, would there be any need to travel towards or anywhere near Rivonia?'

'No. Melrose Arch is south-east of Sandton City, Rivonia is north.'

'Have you ever been to Amanda's cottage in Rivonia?'

A long pause followed before Plaistowe gulped down most of the water in his bottle. 'Only once, when I fetched her for a date about six months ago.'

'I assume it was twice,' said Dlamini, 'once when you fetched her and once when you dropped her off.'

'I didn't drop her off. She took a taxi home.'

'Why?'

'We had an argument over dinner and she walked out on me.'

'What did you argue about?'

'Personal stuff, you know, men and women and dating.'

'I don't know, please enlighten me?'

'It was no big deal. I'm a bit hazy now on what exactly happened.'

He took another sip of water.

Dlamini pushed and prodded cautiously until Plaistowe admitted the fight was about Amanda not being interested in anything more than a platonic relationship.

'But what angered or upset her so much that she abandoned the date?'

'You know women, they can be temperamental,' said Plaistowe, with a collusive smirk.

Again Dlamini pushed and prodded until Plaistowe confessed that he told Amanda to find her own way home.

'Does Mr Bagley-Smith have a nickname around the office?' asked Dlamini, suddenly changing direction.

Plaistowe smiled, pausing before he replied, 'Yes.'

'What was it?'

Another pause. 'The Roving Perv.'

'Why?'

'Do you really want me to answer that?'

'Yes, I do'

Plaistowe looked around the room as if searching for a form of words. He swallowed the last of his water. 'It was a bit of a joke among the younger crowd that he had a lecherous eye for the women.'

'How did he feel about that?'

'He wasn't happy and complained to the managing partners.'

'How do you know he complained?'

'My father told me, and asked about the nickname.'

'While you were in or near the fifth basement at the Egoli Hotel on the night of the staff party did you see or hear either Jeremy or Amanda?'

'No.'

'How did you get home after the party?'

'My father, the chairperson of the firm, took me,' said Plaistowe, with an emphasis on chairperson.

'Are you willing to let us have access to your phone service provider to confirm your movements between 1 a.m. and four o'clock on the Sunday morning?'

'That would be an invasion of my privacy, so the answer's no,' he said emphatically.

'What is your personal opinion of Jeremy Winters?'

'He's okay, I guess. We're not mates.'

'Are you jealous of him?'

Plaistowe laughed. 'Me jealous of him? You must be joking, what on earth for?'

'Because' said Dlamini, 'most people in the firm saw Jeremy as the rising star, the young lawyer who stood out amongst his peers. Isn't that so?'

'I have nothing to be jealous about, I'm comfortable in my own skin, and do I need to remind you that the firm was built by my family—my family, not anyone else.'

'Thank you, that's it, we're done,' said Dlamini. 'I have to wonder, though, how proud you feel, and how proud your father would feel if he knew about your rudeness and arrogance when you arrived here today. Shame on you, young man, shame on you.'

Roger pushed back his chair noisily, raised himself with a childish insolence and swaggered out of the room, bottle in hand.

David Plaistowe arrived ten minutes early for his interview. In contrast to his son, he was courteous and pleasant, greeting Dlamini, and then introducing himself to the rest of the team, and finally to the stenographer.

'I do hope I can be of some help to bring this terrible affair to an end. I'm still shocked at what Winters did to that young woman, and now it's time for him to take responsibility; it's been nearly three months.'

'I've read your statement to the police and want to clarify a few points, if I may,' said Dlamini in a polite tone.

'Please, be my guest,' replied Plaistowe, sitting tall with a ramrod back.

Dlamini walked to a side table and poured a glass of water which he placed on the table next to Plaistowe.

'Thank you, Mr Dlamini, awfully kind of you.'

'Where do you reside?'

'I have quite a few residences here in South Africa and abroad, but I take it you're interested in my Johannesburg place?' asked Plaistowe, unable to stop himself flaunting his wealth.

'Yes,' said Dlamini. 'The residence you were staying at in December last year.'

'It's on Westcliff Ridge, not far from Zoo Lake. We've lived there for about twenty years. It was designed by Sir Herbert Baker for one of the early mining magnates. It has the best view in Johannesburg. You must come and visit us some day and see for yourself.'

'You make me envious,' said Dlamini with a wry smile before pressing on. 'When you took Roger home after the party, which route did you take and what car were you driving?'

Plaistowe took a sip of water and then cleared his throat. 'I'm not sure why you'd want to know something so trivial, but if it's relevant, I drove my Bentley and went south along Oxford Road before cutting east past the Wanderers cricket stadium to Melrose Arch.'

'I assume you took the same journey in reverse when you returned to the hotel to look for your mobile?'

'Yes, that's right.'

'And what was your route after you collected your phone?'

'Straight home, south along Oxford Road before cutting west to Jan Smuts Avenue, past Zoo Lake and the Zoo, and then west again off Jan Smuts onto the Ridge. Look, my good man, I've no problem answering your questions, but I'm rather intrigued why you would want details of my journeys?'

'Over the years I've developed this silly habit of checking all background detail in case something useful pops out,' said Dlamini smiling.

'We are creatures of habit, aren't we?'

'So, to complete this point, from what you've said to the police, and to me, you didn't travel north of Sandton City on either the Saturday night or the Sunday morning of the party?'

'Why would I, there was no need,' he said calmly.

Dlamini changed tack.

'Is it correct that Mr Bagley-Smith complained to the managing partners about the nickname given to him in the office? I understand he was referred to as "The Roving Perv".'

'He did but I disregarded it as silliness on the part of some immature young women.'

Dlamini switched gears again. 'I believe the hotel management informed your marketing and events department about two CCTV cameras being out of order, and that this was passed onto the managing partners. Were you aware of that before the party?'

'Yes, yes, all the managing partners were aware, but we didn't think it was an issue.'

'On the night in question, why did you take the stairs when you returned to collect your phone?'

'I was tired and quite unintentionally parked one level too low.'

'So you would've entered the lobby from the stairwell to get to the bathroom where you left your phone?' asked Dlamini.

'Correct.'

'And because of the broken CCTV cameras, I suppose there won't be any footage of your arrival and departure?'

'Hang on a minute, old chap, what the hell are you suggesting? I've been over all this stuff with Thabani Kumalo who showed me the footage. It's obvious that Winters did this—all the evidence points to him and no one else. I mean, look how he lied to the police.'

'How do you know Winters lied to the police?'

'Kumalo told me.'

'Why did Kumalo share this with you and why did he show you the CCTV footage?'

'It's really quite simple—nothing ominous—as chairperson of the most prominent law firm on the African continent I have to manage public perceptions and to that end I have met with Kumalo periodically to be updated on the investigation. The sooner you tell your client to plead guilty and accept the consequences, the better for all of us—Amanda's family, all the folk at Plaistowe Incorporated, and the public at large.'

'Are you willing to give your consent to us accessing information from your mobile phone service provider, showing your movements in the early hours of Sunday morning?' asked Dlamini.

'What?' exclaimed David Plaistowe, staring down his nose. 'You must be insane if you think I'm going to let anyone invade my privacy.'

'You will understand, I'm sure, that I must cover all the bases. Any objection to us having access to the car you drove to and from the party?'

The effect on Plaistowe was electric. With hunched shoulders he thrust his hands, fingers splayed, towards Dlamini across the boardroom desk.

'Have you gone stark raving mad? You're on a fishing expedition and you know it. The police have done their investigation and I've given them whatever assistance I can. That's it!'

Plaistowe realised he had lost his cool and took a drink of water from the glass at his elbow.

'One last question,' said Dlamini. 'What is your relationship with Detective Captain Kumalo? I know you've taken him on a hunting trip and that he's accompanied you on trips to Mauritius and Cyprus.'

'I expected better from you, Dlamini, that's such a rank amateurish angle and, quite frankly, one that will land you in trouble,' said Plaistowe, regaining his composure.

After David Plaistowe's departure Dlamini bagged a second glass.

Advocate Dlamini's interview with Kumalo revealed nothing significant. The man presented as a tough, seasoned cop who, quite clearly, had been around the block many times. Dlamini focused on Kumalo's apparent reluctance to follow up on obvious potential leads, and on his relationship with Plaistowe senior. The detective shut down the questioning rather quickly, insisting the relationship wasn't improper and refusing to talk about it for reasons he was unwilling to divulge. He added that he didn't see any good reason for following other leads as, in his opinion, and in the opinion of the prosecutor, the case against Jeremy Winters was a slam dunk.

The defence team were both excited and anxious about the remaining two interviews scheduled for the following day, uncertain about what the couple from the accounts department would reveal.

17

On time, Jilly Zandberg and Zara Wolensky, nervously holding hands, arrived together on Friday morning. Jilly volunteered to go first.

Advocate Dlamini canvassed some background information with her, establishing that both she and Zara had worked at Plaistowe's for more than twenty years.

'You're obviously happy at the firm,' said Dlamini.

'Tremendously so,' replied Jilly.

'And loyal?'

'Of course.'

'Such loyalty is a rare attribute nowadays,' said Dlamini, before asking her about her statement to the police. 'Which officer took your statement?'

'Detective Constable Jansen.'

'What was he like in his dealings with you?'

She thought for a while before answering. 'Abrupt and somewhat aggressive.'

'Aggressive how?'

'His tone, attitude and general body language.'

'Besides the two of you, was there anyone else present at the time?' asked Dlamini.

'No, only the two of us. Zara had to wait in another room.'

'In taking your statement, did Jansen ask you questions and did he then record exactly what you said, or did you write out your statement, or was there a different approach?'

'He was only interested in what Jeremy and Amanda did when the elevator stopped at the fifth basement.'

'Did he ask how they were with each other on the way down to the basement?'

'No.'

'When you described to him what they did, did he take down word for word what you said?'

'No, he waited until I finished, and then he typed up that part of the statement using his own words.'

'How did you describe their behaviour when you stopped at level five?'

'I told him they were preoccupied with each other to such an extent that they didn't even realise the elevator doors had opened. I prodded Jeremy on the shoulder and said something like, "Hey Lovebirds, we're here". Jeremy turned to leave, holding Amanda's hand. She expressed concern about what people might think and suggested it would be better if they returned to the party.'

'Go on, what happened then?'

'Jeremy said something along the lines of, "Don't worry about them, they're also having a good time, let's go to the car", and then he pulled Amanda towards the open door. She seemed a bit nervous and stood firm, saying again she was worried about what people would think. He tugged at her, saying she was being silly, and they should go. She then followed him.'

'What did you mean when you said they were preoccupied with each other?'

'Well, they were embracing, kissing and whispering to each other.'

'Did you think Amanda was a reluctant participant?'

'No, she was definitely into him.'

'Had it been like that all the way down?'

'Yes.'

'From your observations, did you think Amanda left the elevator against her will?'

'No. Even though she was concerned about what people might think and initially stood firm, I think she was being more playful than anything else. In fact, when they were about five metres out of the elevator, they were all over each other again.'

Dlamini read to her that part of the statement dealing with Jeremy pulling Amanda out of the elevator. 'Is that a correct record of what you conveyed to Jansen?'

'Not really, because it doesn't capture the context I tried to convey.'

'Thank you, Ms Zandberg, you've been most helpful.'

Zara Wolensky confirmed Jilly Zandberg's version of events and, importantly, her impression that Amanda's reluctance to exit the elevator wasn't seriously meant.

Feet up and leaning back on the pool lounger with a cold beer in hand, Gary reflected on the last ten days. Charlie lay at his feet, grunting softly every time the caring hand stroked his head. Recent events had, at least as far as the defence team was concerned, been promising. The discovery of the missing dress at the cottage was a significant breakthrough, confirming

Amanda had been home, and suggesting strongly, and perhaps even proving, that Jeremy couldn't have killed her. But Gary was all too aware that the investigation was far from over; Jeremy's name wouldn't be cleared until the real killer was found. The defence team, wanting more time to complete investigations, asked the prosecutor for an extended trial date, three months hence. He acceded reluctantly, warning that any further request would not be viewed favourably as that would take them beyond six months since the murder.

Gary turned his attention to the Plaistowes and Bagley-Smith, and wondered whether one of them might be the killer. Roger and Bagley-Smith fared poorly when questioned by Advocate Dlamini, and the movements of all three of them in the early hours of the Sunday morning were suspicious. On the other hand, Gary couldn't rule out the possibility that it was someone else from the party, or one of the other many visitors to the hotel, or even a member of staff, who surreptitiously slipped down the stairs. He cogitated on the various permutations only to confirm to himself that much more evidence was required to finger the perpetrator.

'C'mon, Charlie, time to stretch those stumpy legs of yours, let's go, let's go.'

Needing little encouragement, the dog was up like a shot, scampering to the hallway where his leash hung invitingly on the wall.

They had the park to themselves, so Gary gave him the run of the place. It was a joy to see him relishing the freedom of being unleashed. By the time they reached the stream at the far end of the park, Charlie's panting and lolling tongue bore testimony to having overdone it. He splashed into the shallow water and immersed most of his muscular body.

'Okay, my pal, you've had enough time to cool off; it's time to go home.'

Charlie dragged himself out of the stream, engaging Gary with those bright brown eyes, and turned for home. Too tired to follow Gary into the house, Charlie flopped down in the shade of the pepper tree in the backyard. Gary let him be, knowing he would come in after an hour or so, scrounging for his supper, as he always did. In the meantime Gary had tasks to get on with, not least of all trying to persuade his bank manager for some leeway on his mortgage payments. The manager kept him on the call for more than half an hour, wanting all sorts of information before finally agreeing to suspend payments for three months.

At last, Gary could make the call to Paris he had been looking forward to.

'Oh, how I miss you,' he said when Julia answered. 'It's been too long.'

'Hello, Gary, I'm missing you as well, even though it's only been a few days.'

'It feels much longer. How's the assignment going?'

'Much the same as always—demanding hours and bossy photographers, although one of them is exceptionally nice.'

'How nice?' he asked with a nervous chuckle.

'Are you jealous, big guy? I hope so.'

'Me, jealous? Maybe a tiny bit.'

'Nothing to be concerned about, I promise. How's your father doing, and how's your mum holding up? I know this is a difficult time for you. I wish I could do something to help.'

'Thanks, Jules, I trust you. According to the hospice, Dad's close to the end. My sister and I are giving Mum as much support as she needs, but I fear for her. I'm not sure she'll be able to handle his passing.'

'You guys are in my thoughts and my prayers, know that, Gary. I'm flying back the day after tomorrow and can step in with support if you need a break.'

'That's sweet and considerate of you.'

'Can't wait to see you. How's the case going?'

'We're getting there but we need more evidence. I'm feeling the strain, I guess it's because I'm so close to Jeremy and his family.'

Neither of them wanted to terminate the call, but Julia had to get going to her next shoot. 'Please give adorable Charlie a huge hug from me.'

'Will do. Love you.'

Once the call ended he immediately felt a surge of loneliness, an emotion that now encompassed him every time he was in the house without Julia.

That's strange, he thought, *Charlie hasn't come up for his food.*

Gary called and whistled for him. Usually he would come running immediately, but this time there was no familiar snorting and grunting.

'Well, Charlie, I guess I'll have to come and find you.'

Gary made his way down the stairs, continuing to call and whistle, but still no response. Walking into the backyard, he saw Charlie lying on his side near the pepper tree, head facing towards the gate leading to the park.

'Hey Charlie, c'mon, get up—food time.' He didn't move. 'Hey, my pal, what's wrong with you, come, up you get.'

Still no movement. Gary stepped towards the dog and felt a knot tighten in his stomach. He crouched down, noticing vomit near Charlie's face and what appeared to be a piece of meat on the ground. He shook Charlie and then noticed froth around his mouth. Gary went cold, fearing the worst.

'Charlie, Charlie, what's happened, what's happened?' he cried in anguish, moving closer, seeking signs of life. There weren't any. He let out a guttural scream, before cupping his hands over his mouth trying to stifle the noise. Futilely he softly stroked the lifeless body. 'Oh Charlie, what's going on?'

His mind and body were overcome with numbness. All he could manage in his despair was to stare blankly up at the dark clouds rolling in. Eventually he summoned sufficient energy to return to the house to fetch a blanket in which he carefully wrapped Charlie's unmoving body. He carried the cradled bundle to the car and then drove off to get help. His sadness turned to anger when the vet confirmed Charlie had been poisoned.

His home felt cold, unwelcoming and lonely when he stepped in. He needed someone to talk to, someone with whom he could share his grief and his anger. He tried to call Lucy, but she didn't answer. He then called Julia but when she didn't pick up, he remembered the photo shoot.

For a moment he considered phoning his sister but quickly abandoned the idea. She had more than enough to cope with. *Pull yourself together, Gary Edwards,* he chided himself, reaching into the liquor cabinet for an unopened bottle of whisky. Without thinking he reached for a CD of a Mozart sonata and placed it in the player.

He knew it was morning when the warmth of the rising sun enveloped him. Taking in his surroundings through squinting eyes he noticed the half-empty whisky bottle next to the ice bucket teetering on the edge of the coffee table. Still trying to orientate himself, the intercom buzzed. He slid slowly off the recliner, almost losing his balance as his feet touched the ground. 'Hold on, dammit, I'm coming,' he shouted, unsteady on his feet.

He answered. Lucy was at the security gate.

'Okay, let her in,' he said into the intercom, before unlatching the front door and making his way to the kitchen. His tongue felt rough as it tried to shed the furriness from his mouth.

'What've you been up to, Gary Edwards, you look terrible and stink of booze,' said Lucy.

He rubbed his unshaven chin and looked down at his crumpled clothes. 'What the hell are you doing here?' he asked. 'Everything okay?'

'I think I should be asking you that,' she said. 'Have you forgotten we're meant to be going to the hotel to look at more CCTV footage?'

He glanced at the kitchen clock and saw they had less than forty minutes to get there.

'Dammit, I did forget, and I'm also seeing Snyman later,' he shouted, charging down the passage. 'Help yourself, I shan't be long. I'll explain later.'

On the way to the hotel he told her about Charlie. 'I'm broken, absolutely bloody broken. I tried to call you.'

'I'm so sorry. Who would do such a cruel and terrible thing, and why, and how did they get the poison to Charlie?'

'A poisoned piece of meat was thrown over the back fence from the open park. I've thought about the who and why for most of the night and can only think someone's got it in for me, wanting to send some sort of message. Why else? What other motive could there possibly be?'

He choked up. She stretched across and softly rubbed his upper arm. 'I feel your pain and your anger. I wish I could fix it.'

They drove along in silence for the rest of the journey.

Chris Plumtree was already in reception in conversation with the head of security. Rubin took them through to the viewing room. 'I know it's going to be a long morning for you guys,' he said, 'so I'll let you get on with it. Call me if there's anything you need. I've arranged for refreshments. Have fun.'

Gary told Chris their focus was only on the front lobby and doors. He pushed over photos of Amanda and Bagley-Smith which Lucy had managed to download at the office.

'We want to see if either of these two people left or returned between 11.30 p.m. on Saturday and four on Sunday morning. I know it's going to be slow and tedious, but we've got to do what we've got to do.'

He wasn't wrong; the process dragged on, testing their powers of concentration. They must have been into their fourth or fifth run when Lucy leapt from her chair shouting, 'Stop, stop, Chris. I think I see her.' The footage was reversed and run again. 'Stop,' she yelled. 'There, that's Amanda,' she said, pointing at a petite woman in a short black halter neck dress in a large group about to exit the revolving door.

Although the sighting lasted no more than a few seconds, an enhanced freeze of the image confirmed that it was indeed Amanda, and she was holding a tissue to her head. The time marker showed 1.40 a.m.

'Fantastic, Lucy, well done. We could so easily have missed that,' said Gary.

'Yip, great spot,' agreed Chris, taking a sip from his cool drink.

'What do we take from this?' asked Lucy.

'Well for starters, Amanda left voluntarily, seemingly to go home,' said Gary. 'And this was after Roger and Bagley-Smith had been down to the fifth basement and before David Plaistowe went down after Roger fetched him.'

'So what?' asked Lucy.

'I'm not sure... not sure, not ...' said Gary with his voice trailing off.

'That reminds me,' she said, 'I still need to check the taxi companies. I'll get onto it in the next few days. I'll also check with them if they picked up Bagley-Smith.'

After an exhausting six hours, with many reruns and repeated checks, they called it a day without having seen any sign of Amanda returning or Bagley-Smith leaving.

'I simply can't get my head round this,' said Gary. 'We know Amanda came back, otherwise her body wouldn't have been found in the stairwell. She doesn't appear to have come through the front door, so how did she get to the basement?'

'It's possible we missed her in the crowds pouring through those doors,' offered Chris, looking at each of them in turn. 'It's also possible,' he said, 'she came in through the parkade entrance.'

'But why come back?' asked Lucy.

'Maybe to check on Jeremy,' suggested Chris.

'I think the first question is the how, and then the why,' said Gary. 'If she entered through the parkade entrance it would've been by car or perhaps, if the security guards were slack, by foot. There was no evidence from the parkade footage of any pedestrian traffic.'

'Wasn't there a late car though?' asked Chris. 'I seem to remember one.'

'You're right,' said Gary. 'David Plaistowe came back to fetch his phone. Give me a moment to check my timeline.' He opened his laptop and quickly found what he was looking for. 'Yes, here it is. David Plaistowe's car entered the parkade at 2.58 a.m. But there would've been no reason for him to have Amanda in his car. He took Roger home who lives in the opposite direction.'

'And what about Bagley-Smith?' asked Lucy.

'I suppose we missed him leaving,' replied Gary. 'You saw how difficult it was at times with so many people coming and going. Surely the man's not stupid enough to lie, knowing we could check CCTV footage?'

Lucy took an Uber to the Winters' home so Gary wouldn't be late for his appointment with the P.I.

He found Willem Snyman sitting on his own in the beer garden. 'Not propping up the bar I see,' said Gary, shaking his hand.

'Too bloody crowded. You know what Saturday's like with every man and his dog crowded around the TV watching rugby.'

Gary ordered a beer for himself and another drink for Snyman which kept them going during some inconsequential chat over the next twenty minutes.

'My turn,' said Willem, asking the hovering waiter to bring another round and a plate of potato fries. 'I've looked carefully into Kumalo's lifestyle,' said Snyman, 'and there's absolutely no hint of any lavish spending. He and Plaistowe have met a few more times since their visit to Cyprus. They went to Mauritius one more time, taking wives, and the other visits have been to Plaistowe's game lodge with business associates, and then once to his wine estate in the Cape.'

Gary mulled over the feedback before asking whether Snyman thought Plaistowe was trying to keep Kumalo sweet for some reason.

'It certainly looks that way. Why would a man of Plaistowe's standing spend so much time in the company of a cop, particularly the cop leading the investigation into the rape and murder at his firm's party?'

'It does look suspicious, I have to say.'

'There's something else though,' said Snyman, 'and this is more interesting and somewhat intriguing. My source at Financial Services Intelligence—you know, where Kumalo was posted before—tells me, although he didn't seem a hundred percent certain, that

Plaistowe is a person of interest to Interpol in connection with money laundering activities and that Kumalo might be trying to infiltrate Plaistowe's circle.'

'What! You're kidding me, right?'

'Only passing on what I've picked up.'

'Let me see if I follow this,' said Gary. 'They're using each other. Plaistowe wants to maintain an influence over Kumalo to ensure the investigation into Amanda's murder does as little harm as possible to his firm, and Kumalo is allowing himself to be pulled in by Plaistowe, hoping to gather intelligence for his former bosses.'

'Something like that, but remember we're putting two and two together and hopefully not coming up with five.'

'This is like something from a John le Carré story,' said Gary, picking up a hot, limp chip.

'Who the hang is John le Carré?' asked Snyman.

'One of the greatest spy storytellers ever. I must share with you something Kumalo's sergeant told me. He said Kumalo was refusing to follow up on some obvious leads in the Winters case. He, the sergeant, was extremely frustrated. I wonder whether this is Kumalo's way of gaining Plaistowe's confidence.'

Snyman arched an eyebrow in Gary's direction.

'No,' said Gary. 'It can't be, simply not plausible. I can understand Plaistowe wanting to keep Kumalo sweet; that's his way—power and money and control. But Kumalo taking on the role of money laundering spy? No, that's too much.'

'By all accounts, Kumalo's a smooth operator. Do with it what you will, Mr Lawyer. I merely pass on what I pick up from good sources.'

'Thanks, I'll certainly keep that in mind. Now listen, while I have you on the clock, can I bounce something off you?'

Gary told him about Charlie. 'Why would anyone want to poison him?'

'Had he perhaps upset neighbours in some way? You know, barking excessively or provoking their pets.'

'Nothing like that,' said Gary. 'Charlie was well behaved and never caused any hassles. Besides, I know everyone in the estate and they're decent sort of people. Certainly not the kind who would poison dogs. I'm sure if they had any problems with Charlie they would've been in touch.'

'Have you made any enemies recently?'

Gary pondered the question. 'I guess a few, but how would they even know about Charlie?'

'Well, that's where I'd look. I think someone's trying to send you a message. Perhaps in passing you've talked about Charlie and how much he meant to you.'

Snyman asked for a lift to Wanderers Sports Club to meet up with some friends.

On approaching the black Ferrari, the P.I. whistled. 'My, my, my, what a beauty. Not many of those around. Obviously, my fees are too low or yours are too high.'

'It took a lot of saving, believe me, but it's worth every cent.'

'Hey, what happened here?' said Snyman, crouching near the passenger door.'

'Don't joke, Willem.'

'I'm dead serious.'

Gary rushed over and squatted down to take a closer look. A deep gouge ran down the side of the car.

'Someone's keyed it. Can you believe this, some horrible jerk has keyed my car,' croaked Gary, hands on hips. 'I'll kill the swine if I catch him.'

He rubbed at the scar, dislodging fresh curls of flaking paint.

'First Charlie, now my Ferrari. What's next?'

18

Driving into the glare of the late afternoon sun, Gary headed to the forensic lab. This was a big day. Myriad thoughts danced through his head, some about the case, others about his uncertain future, and the rest about his beloved Charlie. For a moment he became philosophical and then began to wonder about the evidence on the case and whether forensics had found anything significant. He hoped so. He then reflected on Snyman's revelation and the possibility that Plaistowe and Kumalo were playing each other. *Could it be? Improbable, me thinks.*

As he rounded the corner with the laboratory in sight, he had a fleeting, sickening thought. *Is it possible that Jeremy killed Amanda when she returned?* He quickly admonished himself for even thinking it. *Why would he, when she came to check on him?*

He was rather surprised there had been no recent contact from Kumalo or Pillay. It had been many weeks since they made available the dress with shoulder straps and Kumalo had insisted on Pillay having it examined again by a different expert. Something wasn't right.

The team was already waiting in the conference room. Gary took the empty seat next to Lucy, smelling her familiar perfume as he leaned over.

'By the way, do you know if anyone at the office knew about my Charlie?' he whispered.

'Of course, you talked about him often.'

'Really?'

'Yes, really, Gary. Why do you ask?'

'I'll tell you later, the briefing's about to start.'

After distributing copies of the forensic report, the lead examiner summarised the findings before running through it paragraph by paragraph. The only stains on the halter neck dress were Jeremy's semen, and a small blood stain at the top left front side. 'We matched that stain to the victim,' said the examiner. 'It probably came from the injury to her head.'

He then considered the other dress. 'Now this is rather interesting. There were no stains on this dress, but we found minute, and I mean really microscopic, traces of two different carpet fibres. One sample of fibres, which were dark blue, matched those taken from the carpet in the cottage. They were found only on the back of the dress, with traces at the top, roughly in the middle, and at the hem.'

'What, if anything, does that tell us?' asked Advocate Dlamini.

'We are of the opinion that the wearer of that dress was at some point lying on her back on the carpet in question,' said the examiner.

'Could the fibres not have been picked up if the dress, without being worn, was laid out on the carpet?' asked Gary.

'No, there had to be some downward pressure,' replied the examiner before turning to the other fibres. 'These were dark grey in colour and spread down the right side of the dress, suggesting the wearer was lying on her right side on a carpet. We had no carpet sample for comparison purposes.'

'Could that carpet have been in a vehicle?' asked Dlamini.

'Certainly,' said the examiner.

The group learned that a small blood stain on the left breast pocket of Amanda's dressing gown also came from her, and that there were only two matches from the many fingerprints lifted. Most of those were Amanda's prints, but one partial print taken from a tap in the bathroom matched the prints on one of the glasses bagged by Dlamini.

'And which glass was that?' asked Gary excitedly.

The examiner looked down at the report. 'The glass is identified as Bagley-Smith.'

Gary let out a soft whistle. 'This becomes more and more intriguing,' he said, before asking whether there was any way of knowing how old the partial print was.

'Unfortunately, not. Prints can last for many months, even longer.'

'To be sure, were there fingerprints that didn't match Amanda's?' asked Dlamini.

'Yes, quite a number. We've no way of knowing to whom those belong. Probably family, friends, cleaners, etcetera.'

'No match to the prints on the bottle provided to you?' questioned Dlamini.

'No match,' replied the examiner.

After the briefing the forensics team left, leaving the others to consider the findings.

'How fascinating,' said Dlamini. 'Let's spend a bit of time going over the material points. Gary, won't you take us through those?'

'Here we go, in random order,' said Gary, reading from his laptop notes.

'Access to Amanda before departing from the basement – Jeremy, Roger Plaistowe and Bagley-Smith.

Access also possible via the stairwell for other hotel visitors, other party guests and hotel staff. Why use stairs? No knowledge of defective cameras?

Amanda's intimacy towards Jeremy.

Amanda left hotel at 1.40 a.m., and her dress was changed before she returned. Why return? Why change dress? How did she return? Why did police not notice change of dress or were they aware?

Bagley-Smith's lewd comments and his reputation for leering at young women. Also, his fingerprint at the cottage. N.B., he did give her a lift home when she worked late and may have used bathroom.

When did Bagley-Smith leave the hotel and where did he go?

Did David take Roger home before he returned supposedly to collect his phone?

The relationship between Kumalo and David Plaistowe

Kumalo's reticence to follow leads.

Did the lone woman, Carol Ibbets, recognise the man's voice in the basement?

Odd movements of David and Roger in the basements.

Carpet fibres on the shoulder-strap dress.

Neck of champagne bottle wiped clean. Why would Jeremy do that?

David Plaistowe's car – the only one to enter the parkade after Amanda left the hotel. How do we access his car to check for any Amanda DNA and examine carpets?

How do we access tracker and mobile phone information for the Plaistowes and Bagley-Smith?'

'Clearly the prosecution case against Jeremy is weak,' commented Dlamini, 'and absent further compelling evidence against him coming to light the charges are bound to fail.'

Lucy nudged Gary and smiled.

'I agree,' said Gary, 'but we need to get beyond that. Our client's name will forever be sullied unless the real killer is found. Who do you think it is, Herbert?' asked Gary.

'I have my suspicions, but that's as far as it goes. There's insufficient evidence to implicate anyone in particular. I think the ring of suspicion could shrink markedly if you could check vehicle and mobile phone movements for the Plaistowes and Bagley-Smith and conduct a forensic sweep of Plaistowe senior's car.'

'But how do we get access?' asked Gary.

'Short of asking a judge, you don't,' said Dlamini, stating the obvious. 'Perhaps you could start with the traffic department to see if there's any helpful street camera footage.'

As they entered the car park a uniformed police officer intercepted them, asking for Gary.

'That's me,' he said.

'Mr Edwards, I'm Constable Jorges. A charge of aggravated assault has been laid against you by a Mr Roger Plaistowe. Please will you accompany me to Sandton City police station. If you don't come voluntarily, I'll have to arrest you.'

Knowing the story of how Gary had assaulted Roger Plaistowe shortly after Jeremy's arrest, Advocate Dlamini identified himself.

'Hello Advocate Dlamini, I know who you are,' said the officer. 'I've seen you in court many times.'

'Look, officer, I'm sure we can deal with this without any fuss. We'll follow you back to the station. Is that okay?'

'Of course,' replied the officer.

'By the way, how did you know Mr Edwards was here?' asked Dlamini.

'I got a call about forty minutes ago from the complainant.'

Lucy and the others closed in around Gary as they walked to the cars.

'Roger's having me followed,' said Gary. 'I'm now convinced he's behind the killing of Charlie and the keying of the car. I predict the next thing's going to be a civil action claiming damages for the assault.'

Lucy in her usual caring way slipped her hand into his and whispered, 'You're more than enough for that pathetic wimp, hang in there.'

He squeezed her hand and smiled. 'Ask yourself why is Roger doing these things,' he said.

The visit to the police station turned out to be rather uneventful, aided by the presence of Advocate Dlamini. After capturing Gary's personal details and reading him his constitutional rights he was invited to make a statement which he declined to do other than to say his rights were fully reserved. Constable Jorges informed him he would be contacted in due course about a court appearance date.

'I think we should head out to Jeremy to let him know what's going on,' suggested Gary. 'I won't be able to stay long.'

'I know he'll be waiting for feedback from our meeting,' said Lucy. 'I'll follow you because I'm staying on for dinner. By the way, why did you want to know whether anyone at the office knew about Charlie?'

'The person who poisoned him must've known Charlie was my dog.'

Jeremy was full of praise for Gary's sterling investigative work and his many sacrifices thus far. 'I'm so tempted to break open a bottle of champers, but I'll restrain myself for a while longer,' he said. 'But that doesn't mean I'm not grateful.' He gave his friend a prolonged hug. 'I don't have the words to express how I feel, but know this, I'll always be indebted to you and I'll never, to my dying day, forget what you've done for me.'

'I've done no more than you would've done for me if the roles were reversed.'

'Shouldn't we approach the prosecution now with what we've uncovered and ask them to drop the charges?' asked Jeremy.

'We could,' said Gary, 'but my instincts tell me it's too soon. There are some loose ends I want to tie up first so we can show, not only your innocence but, importantly for your reputation's sake, who the real culprit is.'

'How confident are you about finding the real killer?' asked Jeremy.

'We're getting close. Hopefully, it won't be much longer.'

Gary readied himself to leave.

'I'm sorry about Charlie and your expensive car,' said Jeremy. 'That's too awful.'

He put on a brave face. 'Thank you. Not a nice thing, but woe betide the shithead when I find him.'

'I bet,' said Jeremy, giving him a gentle slap on the shoulder.

Before Gary reached the internal garage door into his house, spicy aromas wafted over him. He could hear singing above the cranked music. He slipped in quietly, creeping up behind Julia who was leaning over the cooker.

He clenched her in a hug, bringing his mouth to her ear. 'And who is this strange woman in my kitchen?'

He felt her chest thumping as she screamed out with fright. 'Gary Edwards, that wasn't funny! You could've killed me.'

She turned, stretched her arms around his neck, and kissed him. 'Oh, I missed you so much. I'm finding it harder and harder to be away from you.'

She kissed him again but more passionately this time. They clung on to each other, savouring the moment of intimacy. When she let go, he patted her behind.

'I missed you too,' he said, holding both her hands in his and looking into her eyes. 'And you look as good in an apron as you do in swimwear.'

'Me thinks you like the skimpy shorts and braless look,' came the retort.

'I like everything about you, Julia, you're a special person. I thought we were meant to be eating out tonight.'

'We were, but I figured we'd enjoy the night in with my cooking, great red wine, romantic music and...' she paused and winked before continuing, 'and the best desert you've ever had.'

Surfacing after nine the following morning, he stumbled out of bed, leaving Julia stretched across the duvet. While waiting for the coffee percolator to get done he wandered through to the study. He had left his desk cleared, so he was surprised to see an official looking document beneath a paperweight, seemingly awaiting his attention. A civil summons. *So, Roger Bloody Plaistowe is at it again.*

19

'Hi, Gary, got your voice message. What's up?' asked Snyman.

'Willem, thanks for getting back. A couple of things. Although I'm still being followed, I've had no more nasty incidents, so I think you can pull your guy off.'

'Will do, and the other things?'

'I think I know who had Charlie killed and my car keyed.' Gary brought him up to speed on the criminal charge and civil summons initiated by Roger Plaistowe. 'It seems too much of a coincidence to have these four incidents happen in quick succession.'

'You may well be right. How about a bit of payback? I know some guys who don't mind breaking legs.'

Gary chuckled and politely declined. 'Look, the main purpose for being in touch is to find out how well you're connected at the traffic department.'

'Pretty well. I'm owed a few favours. What are you after?'

Gary explained his need to see street camera footage for the main roads leading from Sandton City to Rivonia and from Sandton City to Melrose Arch.

'What specifically do you want to check?'

'Whether a particular car, a Bentley, travelled on the Rivonia route or the Melrose Arch route in either or both directions on the night in question.'

'Sounds intriguing, tell me more.'

After Gary filled in the blanks, Snyman said, 'Leave it with me for a few days, but keep your expectations in check. Most of the street cameras are pretty rubbish. In case we get lucky, send me the registration number of the Bentley.'

'Will do,' said Gary.

Without confirmation from the street cameras, Gary's only chance of checking David Plaistowe's journeys would be through his car tracker and mobile phone service providers. He knew all too well that that was unlikely because a judge would have to approve, and it was more likely His Lordship would insist the matter be left to the police. And what about the movements of Roger Plaistowe and Bagley-Smith? Same problem. Depending on their movements they could either be eliminated from suspicion or the net could tighten. *I have no choice; I must somehow get hold of this information. But how?*

Perhaps it was time to take Detective Sergeant Pillay into his confidence.

Meanwhile he could take a breather from the case for the rest of the week, except to give Elaine Shelton feedback on the forensics. Gary settled into thinking about his future career plans. He sensed, and hoped, it wouldn't be much longer before his defence team commitments would be something of the past. He was clear about one thing: he had no intention of returning to his former firm, regardless of what they offered. The more he thought about it the more he liked the idea of he and Jeremy starting their own practice. They would hit it off, he had no doubt, and they could bring in some of the young stars in the city and build something unique, avoiding many of the failings of the bigger firms.

Finally Friday rolled around, the day he had planned for the perchance meeting with Lucy and Carol Ibbets. Before he left the house he got a call from Snyman.

'Hey, Willem, I wasn't expecting to hear from you so soon. What's up?'

'Both good news and bad news.'

'Hold on, I want to grab my note pad.' He sat down at the study desk, switching his phone to speaker mode.

'Let's have the bad news first,' he said.

'The cameras along the Rivonia route weren't working on the weekend of the party. They're still broken. Typical bloody municipality.'

'And the good news?'

'Believe it or not, the cameras on the Melrose Arch route did work that weekend.'

'That's brilliant. Any sign of the Bentley?' He crossed his index and middle fingers on the right hand.

'That's the other bit of good news,' said the P.I. 'The Bentley was picked up by the cameras in both directions.'

'At what times?' asked Gary, cutting in impatiently.

'Between 3.15 and 3.28 for the trip to Melrose Arch and from 3.42 to 3.54 for the return trip. When the car got to Oxford Road though, it didn't head back to Sandton City but instead went in the opposite direction.'

'Are you sure? No sign of the car on that route before three o'clock?'

'Absolutely sure,' said Snyman. 'Does any of this mean anything, Gary?'

'Damn sure it does. It means David Plaistowe has lied about his movements that morning. According to him he took his son to Melrose Arch sometime around 2 a.m. and then returned immediately to the hotel to collect his mobile. The cameras show him going to Melrose Arch about an hour later and not returning to the hotel. By heading in the opposite direction when he got to Oxford Road he would've been going home.'

'But why lie about this?'

'Simple. He had to fit in with the timings on the hotel CCTV footage and parkade registers. The hotel records show him leaving the first time at six minutes past two and returning at two minutes to three. He leaves again fourteen minutes later and drives to Melrose Arch. Where did he go that first time?'

'Did the hotel CCTV footage show anyone in the car with Plaistowe?'

'No, definitely not,' replied Gary.

'And the first time he left?'

'The CCTV shows Roger in the vehicle with his father.'

'It seems that on the first trip Roger and his father went somewhere other than to Roger's apartment. Let me check the street camera shots again to see whether Plaistowe was on his own.'

Gary pushed his way through the rowdy beer garden crowd. After scouting around he eventually spotted Lucy and Carol.

'Hello, Lucy, imagine seeing you here,' he said with feigned surprise.

'Hey, Gary, how are things? Have you met Carol?'

'Actually, I haven't. Hi, Carol. I saw you at the office a few times before I left.'

She returned the greeting with a smile at the same time dropping her chin ever so slightly towards the side of her chest.

'What are you doing here?' asked Lucy.

'I'm meant to be meeting a friend, but he called a couple of minutes ago to say his car's broken down. Hopefully he won't be too long.'

'Why don't you join us while you wait?' suggested Lucy. 'You don't mind do you, Carol?'

'Not at all,' she replied, gesturing with her hand for him to take a seat.

'How did your meeting go with Amanda's mother?' asked Lucy.

'Okay, I guess. She was understandably still emotional, but grateful for the feedback. She again promised not to tell her husband. She sends her regards.'

After more than an hour and a few drinks under their belts Gary pretended to call his friend. 'No, he's not going to make it.'

Surprisingly it was Carol who invited him to stay on. 'It's good to get to know the person I've heard so much about round the office.'

'Probably all bad,' he said.

'Depends on who you talk to,' she said with a slight slur, beating Lucy to the draw. Gary and Lucy glanced fleetingly at each other, realising Carol was a bit drunk. She continued. 'Most people I talk to say wonderful things—that you're a brilliant lawyer, you're going places—and the women, well...' She let her words hang in the air as a cheeky smile crossed her lips.

'Oh, you're just saying nice things, so sweet of you,' said Gary with an equally flirtatious hint to his voice.

'Hey, you two, shall I leave?' asked Lucy with a chuckle. They all laughed and then Carol carried on where she left off. 'But amongst the managing partners, not so nice.'

'You know why, don't you? All because I did the honourable and decent thing of standing up for an innocent young guy whose reputation was being torn to shreds by false accusations.'

'So, I've been told,' said Carol.

'I'm afraid too few people have the courage of their convictions. It cost me my partnership, and that was a small price to pay for doing what was and is right,' he said, looking straight at her.

Not wanting to push too hard too soon he asked her about her time in Canada. She became emotional and said she longed for her mother most, but also for some of her close friends, as well as the simple pleasures of Canadian efficiency.

'And how are you enjoying the firm?' he asked.

'Love the people—so friendly and welcoming.'

'And the job?'

'I suppose like all jobs, some good and some bad. A bit restrictive for me because of my dad's relationship with Mr Plaistowe.'

'I believe you've met Detective Captain Kumalo a few times—nice man,' said Gary.

'I've only seen him at some of Mr Plaistowe's functions and I've had to make travel and accommodation bookings for him when he travels overseas with the boss.'

'A bit of an odd situation, don't you think?' asked Gary. 'One of the wealthiest and most powerful men around mixing with a cop. And not any old cop, but the one leading the murder investigation.'

'I don't ask questions, and do what I'm told. It's easier that way. Besides, I'm lucky to earn the salary I earn, and boy, do I need it.'

It was now or never. 'Carol, I need your help. Jeremy needs your help. You're the only person that stands between him clearing his good name and his whole career going up in flames.'

She turned to him with an expressionless face.

'I believe you know what I'm referring to.' He paused and then continued. 'Did you recognise the voice of the man who shouted at Amanda in the basement?'

She hesitated so long that he thought she wasn't going to answer. He waited patiently.

'I've already told Lucy what I know. I'm going to land myself in deep, deep trouble if I carry on talking about it,' she said, looking away.

'Carol, look at me,' said Gary. 'I'll only use what you tell me if you agree. You have my word. Did you recognise the man? Please, Carol. Jeremy's running out of time.'

She shuffled in her seat and chewed at a fingernail. 'I need the loo.'

'So do I,' said Lucy. 'You can order us another round of drinks, Mr Edwards,' said Lucy with a frown.

He wondered whether he should push harder. Getting a positive identification would, he believed, unlock the entire mystery.

On their return to the table Carol was more unsteady on her feet and her complexion had taken on a pallid tone.

'I trust you girls won't mind but I've ordered us a selection of tapas. I'm famished.'

'That's what I need,' mumbled Carol. 'I've been drinking too quickly'.

'I think all of us have,' said Lucy supportively.

He didn't prod her for a response to his plea, and again waited patiently. She tackled the food with gusto, wiping away the occasional dribble down the side of her mouth.

Eventually she answered. 'I don't mean to be difficult or unhelpful, but you don't know my old man. His aggression knows no bounds. I can't say any more.'

Gary leaned forward, reaching out to Carol's hands. He took hold of them gently. 'That tells me you did recognise the voice. Don't you understand, you could save a young man from spending the rest of his life in prison? Surely you know the high regard in which Jeremy was held before the firm abandoned him and the press slandered him left, right and centre?'

She withdrew her hands and shook her head. They all ate in silence.

'You do know we can force you to give evidence, and I guess you know what it means not to tell the truth under oath?'

He wondered whether he had gone too far.

She glared at him and got up, threw some cash on the table, and left, stumbling her way out of the beer garden.

'Well, I guess I messed that up,' said Gary.

'I don't think so,' Lucy replied. 'You had to get tough at some point, the gentle approach wasn't going to work. Who knows, she might still come around.'

'A last resort may be to get the police to lean on her if I can persuade them to do their work properly.'

He shared Snyman's revelations about Kumalo and David Plaistowe and told her the news about David's movements after the party. 'Perhaps it's time to use this as leverage against Kumalo. I'll see what Pillay thinks.'

'If you're not going anywhere, why don't we call Jeremy and Julia to join us?' said Lucy.

'Julia's away again, but call Jeremy.'

After the call, Lucy's smile said it all. 'And how're things between the two of you?' he asked.

There was that smile again. 'Great, absolutely wonderful.'

'Getting serious?'

'I think so. You and Julia?'

'Good times. Her career takes her away often, but I guess absence makes the heart grow fonder.'

'How serious?'

'More than casual and less than playing house,' he replied evasively.

Jeremy arrived at the beer garden looking relaxed. Gary allowed him a moment to settle before telling him about Carol's reaction.

'We don't need her to get you off the hook, pal, but her cooperation will almost certainly help us find the killer. But if she won't tell what she knows there are other routes we can follow. It'll take longer though.'

He also enlightened Jeremy about the street camera information and the possibility of putting pressure on the police to step in on some further investigations.

'Such as?' asked Jeremy.

'A forensic sweep of Plaistowe's Bentley, access to tracker and mobile phone data to verify movements, and perhaps take a statement from Carol.'

Lucy gave Jeremy's arm an encouraging squeeze. He acknowledged by caressing her hand.

The loving interaction filled Gary with a mixture of joy and longing: joy that his friend was emerging from the darkness, and longing for the absent Julia. He raised a glass in a toast. 'Here's to the two of you.'

Gary's phone pinged with a message from Snyman. "More info on the Bentley, will be in touch."

20

Snyman called as promised, confirming the Bentley had a passenger on the trip to Melrose Arch but not on the return journey.

'How close to the Egoli Hotel is the first camera where the passenger was spotted?' asked Gary.

'As the hotel is off the main route, the first camera only came into play after about four hundred metres and by that point the passenger was already in the car.'

'So, somewhere in those four hundred metres, David must've picked up Roger. I wonder where.'

They agreed that laying their hands on the missing information had become a priority. Where did the Bentley go on the first trip and why? Snyman said he would do more ferreting and revert if he discovered anything useful.

Meanwhile Gary convened a meeting of the entire defence team, including Jeremy. He updated them on recent developments and canvassed their thoughts on the way forward.

'I have my doubts that our P.I. is going to discover anything further, so we now have to pressurise the police or prosecution to follow up on some paths of enquiry.'

Advocate Dlamini agreed.

'I'm not sure which way to go,' said Gary. 'We could confront Kumalo but, given his cosy relationship with David Plaistowe, that might be risky. Alternatively we could meet with the prosecutor, perhaps together with Kumalo. There's also another route, and that's to go to the press.'

All eyes turned to Dlamini. 'I think the press is out,' he said. 'From a risk perspective, there's no difference whether you confront Kumalo or the prosecutor or both. Whichever way you go, Kumalo will learn about it.'

'I have to say, I would prefer to meet with Kumalo on my own,' said Gary. 'I do wonder though whether he'll follow up by accessing cellphone and tracker data and having a forensic sweep done on the Bentley.'

'He would be a damn fool if he didn't,' replied Dlamini. 'He must know we could make life terribly difficult for him. We could complain to IPID and meet with the prosecutor and we would be justified in applying to court to get access to the phone and tracker records. The press would have a field day.'

'Who or what is IPID?' asked Lucy.

'The Independent Police Investigative Directorate, a government agency responsible for dealing with complaints against the police,' said Dlamini.

Lucy had made some of her own enquiries. She had investigated the possibility that Amanda and Bagley-Smith used taxis after the party. 'Fortunately only two taxi companies operated from the hotel and both have been around for years. I've spoken to all the drivers who picked up passengers outside the hotel in the early hours and showed them photos of Amanda and the Roving Perv.'

Lucy paused, scratching around in a folder.

'And?' asked Gary impatiently.

'No one remembered Bagley-Smith,' she said, 'but one driver had a clear recollection of Amanda. Sorry, hold a moment while I dig out my notes. Okay, here we go. He confirmed picking her up at 1.43 a.m. and dropping her off at her Rivonia address shortly before two.'

'How come he remembered her?' asked Dlamini.

'He said she was upset, crying a lot on the way home. He was concerned because she was bleeding from a cut on her head. He asked whether she needed any help, but all she wanted was to get home as quickly as possible to take a shower.'

'Any return trip?' enquired Gary.

'None of the drivers picked up a passenger in Rivonia after midnight.'

'I'm not surprised,' said Dlamini. 'There was no reason for Amanda to return to the hotel at that time of the morning except, possibly, to check on Jeremy, and if Jeremy had raped her, it would make no sense for her to go back to him.'

'Won't the prosecution argue that Jeremy could've raped her when she returned?' questioned one of the other team members.

'That won't wash,' said Dlamini. 'According to the taxi driver she had already sustained the head injury when he took her home. Also, importantly, we know from the stain on the halter neck dress that Jeremy had sex with Amanda before she left for home.'

'I'm a little lost,' said the same team member.

Gary and Dlamini began to answer at the same before Dlamini invited Gary to continue.

'I was going to say that it's more and more beginning to look like Amanda was forcibly brought back to the hotel.'

'My thoughts exactly,' interjected Dlamini. 'I'll go further and suggest—only my theory, mind you—that someone wanted to stage a murder in the hotel basement and to that end had to bring Amanda's body back to the hotel.'

Gary nodded in agreement as the group remained silent.

Jeremy spoke next. 'Why, why would anyone want to do that?'

'To point the finger at you,' replied Gary. 'You were an easy target given your public display of affection for each other.'

The following day, figuring there was nothing to be gained by speaking to Pillay, Gary decided instead to face up to Kumalo. He took a chance, pitching up at Kumalo's office without an appointment, believing a telephone call or an email would be an utter waste of time.

Kumalo stormed down to the front desk after the duty officer announced Gary's arrival. 'What the hell are you doing here?' he bellowed. 'You can't come barging in here whenever you feel like it, Mr Clever Lawyer, so why don't you get into that fancy little sports car of yours and bugger off.'

He turned his back but before he progressed too far down the passage Gary fired back in his own booming voice.

'You messed up, Captain Kumalo, you've got the wrong dress and the wrong guy. You missed the stained dress.'

Kumalo stopped, turned around and walked slowly back to the front desk. 'What did you say?' he asked, spitting out the question with a glare.

'I said you messed up because you have the wrong dress,' he replied, deliberately emphasising each word.

'That's what I thought you said. What do you mean we missed the stained dress?'

'Exactly that, and there's a lot more. You have the wrong man, Captain. If you let me come to your office, I'll explain.'

Amidst much muttering, Kumalo begrudgingly beckoned him through.

'Well, here we are, I'm listening.'

Gary opened his laptop and showed Kumalo the CCTV footage of Amanda and Jeremy entering the elevator.

'You'll notice that Amanda Shelton is wearing a halter neck dress with a low cut back.'

He froze the frame, allowing Kumalo all the time he needed to grasp the significance of the dress.

'So what?' said Kumalo.

Gary slid over copies of the photographs from the police docket. 'The dress your team photographed at the scene and which you took into your possession is different. Look closely. You'll see it has straps on the shoulders and a high back.'

Kumalo examined the photographs over and over and then asked to see the footage again. His face puffed up and the familiar twitching manifested itself once again. He shut the laptop screen forcefully before rushing to his office door. He flung it open, shouting down the corridor, 'Pillay get your bloody arse in here, now!'

Kumalo slammed the door shut, shaking the dry walls of his office, before hastily returning to the desk and throwing himself into his chair. He glared again.

'This doesn't prove a damn thing. Your client was found half-naked near the deceased and his DNA was under her nails and in her vagina, and he lied to us.'

Pillay entered, mouthing no words like a fish struggling for air. Eventually he said, 'You called, Captain.'

At Kumalo's request Gary shared the evidence with Pillay. He gasped. 'You've got to be kidding. How can that possibly be?'

Gary's revelation unleashed varying speculative responses from both detectives about how, why and when the dresses might have been switched, including the possibility that Amanda had both dresses at the hotel. Gary put paid to the last suggestion, informing them of the evidence showing otherwise.

'This still doesn't change a thing,' spat Kumalo. 'Your client did it and he knows he did it. I don't know offhand how the dresses came to be changed but I'm sure in time we'll find out.'

Gary shared further significant discoveries, careful to omit the relationship between Kumalo and David Plaistowe and the possibility that Carol Ibbets could identify the man who shouted at Amanda when she refused his sexual advances.

'So, here's what we have,' said Gary. 'Amanda left the hotel at 1.40 a.m. on Sunday morning. She was clearly alive, wearing the halter neck dress. This was two hours and ten minutes after she and Jeremy left the party for the fifth basement. He could not have killed her.'

'But,' offered Pillay, 'he could've done so when she returned.'

'That's about as convincing as the views of the Flat Earth Society,' said Gary. 'Why would she leave at such a late hour, change her dress and return voluntarily to the person who must already have made his intentions known to her? And what would his motive be for killing her?'

'What then is your theory, Mr Edwards?' spat Kumalo, jutting his chin.

'I have a good idea what went down, but first I think there are now some obvious leads you should follow up. I'm confident they'll help you identify the real killer.'

'You do now, do you?' said Kumalo sarcastically. 'And what may those be?'

'For starters you should use mobile phone and tracker information to check the detailed movements of the Plaistowes and Bagley-Smith.'

'Why, what justification is there for such steps?'

'You've got to be joking,' replied Gary.

'I don't joke about these sorts of things,' said Kumalo.

Gary banged his fist on the table with frustration as he raised his voice. 'Then open your damn eyes. Look at the totality of the available evidence: the hotel CCTV footage, the street camera footage, the statements of these three gentlemen to the police and to Advocate Dlamini, the report of our forensic experts, the fact that David Plaistowe has already lied about his movements, and Bagley-Smith's lewd comments concerning Amanda.'

'You're jumping to conclusions,' said Kumalo.

'And I'm beginning to think you're intent on nailing Jeremy,' said Gary. 'Has someone got a hold on you, Captain Kumalo?'

A long silence followed before Kumalo rose, almost in slow motion, to his full height. 'How dare you?' he roared. 'You don't know what or who you're messing with, Mr Edwards. Get out of my office, now.'

'Don't threaten me, Captain. And by the way, I also think you should do a forensic sweep of David Plaistowe's Bentley—the one he drove to and from the party. It will be interesting to see whether any of the fibres found on Amanda's dress—you know, the unstained dress—came from his car. And who knows, you might even find a blood stain or two.'

Gary snatched up his laptop. 'Don't duck what's staring you in the face, Captain, it could end badly for you. Terribly badly.'

'And don't you threaten me,' screamed Kumalo, as Gary disappeared down the corridor.

Kumalo launched an attack against Pillay as he hovered over him. 'How the hell did you miss that, Pillay? You've made a fool of us.'

Pillay tried to respond but Kumalo would have none of it. 'Shut up when I'm talking, man, shut up! You've stuffed up the case and you're going to fix it, otherwise you'll be out of this department.'

When it seemed Kumalo was done for the moment, Pillay spoke. 'I'm sorry, Captain, but it's an understandable oversight. All of us missed it, and you can see why. Those dresses are almost identical. We, everyone on the team, including you, watched the CCTV footage many times.'

'Stop with the bloody excuses. I've had enough. You're the lead detective and so you're responsible.' Plucking up courage, Pillay lifted his lanky figure out of the chair, coming close enough to Kumalo to feel his warm breath on his face.

'That's not fair, Captain. I tried, many times, to follow up various leads, including those now suggested by Edwards, and you stopped me. You said we had enough evidence to send Winters to prison for the rest of his life.'

'That was before I knew you overlooked vital evidence.'

'Again, my sincere apologies. No harm done though. Had we known back then what we know now we would've done exactly what we must now do. At worst, we've lost a bit of momentum.'

'You don't see it do you, Pillay? You've embarrassed me and you've brought shame on this department. Go away and think carefully about doing the right thing.'

'Which is what, Captain?'
'Resigning, and don't do another damn thing on this case unless I tell you to.'

21

After three days of silence Gary called Pillay for an update on the police investigation.

'Hey, Dhanraj, what's up, you sound miffed?'

'That's an understatement if ever there was one,' replied Pillay. 'You could've warned me, and now my job's on the line. I thought we had mutual respect and more than a mere passing relationship.'

Gary explained that he had contemplated speaking to him first but decided not to for fear of putting him on the spot.

'Believe me, there never was any intention to blindside you. Quite frankly I wanted to confront Captain Kumalo cold, to test his reaction to the new evidence.'

'Why?'

'Remember you told me about how he had been turning a blind eye to obvious leads; well, I think I've found out why. Your boss isn't quite who he makes himself out to be.'

'You're speaking in riddles. What are you saying?'

'Look, things are at a delicate stage, so I can't say more now, but I'll tell all as soon as it's possible. Has Kumalo moved forward on the leads? I haven't heard from him.'

'Why not ask him yourself? Hold on, I'll put you through,' he said without waiting for a response.

Kumalo came on the line almost immediately, in an uncharacteristic cheery voice.

For a moment Gary was stunned. 'Wow, Captain Kumalo, that's a pleasant surprise; you're usually irritated when we talk.'

'My apologies, Mr Edwards, but as you can imagine, this position brings its own pressures and sometimes they get to me.'

His reconciliatory tone set off alarm bells for Gary.

'I guess you're following up on our last meeting,' said Kumalo. 'I've taken your comments on board but haven't been able to do anything yet and won't get there for a few more days.'

'Are you saying that you're going to follow up the leads, but not just yet?' asked Gary.

'Yes, that's it. I'm caught up in something else which has to be given priority. I wish I could say more, but I can't. If you haven't heard from me within four days get in touch.'

'Okay, Captain, I'm taking you at your word and hope I won't be disappointed. I'm also under pressure as the trial date creeps closer and I would prefer not to take other steps. I'm sure you know what I mean.'

The anticipated explosion from Kumalo didn't materialise; instead he maintained his cheeriness as he bade Gary goodbye.

The familiar ring tone jerked Gary from sleep. He stretched across Julia, wondering how he had ended up sleeping on the wrong side of the bed. Ignoring her gentle groans, he grabbed the phone off the bedside table. It was a stuttering Mr Winters. All Gary could make out was that someone had been arrested. His thoughts immediately turned to Jeremy.

'Slow down there, Mr Winters. We have a bad connection. Repeat what you said.'

By this time Julia was awake, frowning and wiping her eyes.

'Sorry to phone so early, but have you heard the news?' asked Mr Winters.

'No, what news?'

'David Plaistowe's been arrested—in the last half an hour.'

'What! By whom and for what?' asked Gary.

'I don't know. I assumed in connection with the murder.'

'Let me make some calls. I'll get back to you.'

Before he could dial there was another incoming call. Ashley Dobson from *The Chronicle*.

'I assume you've heard,' she said.

'Heard what?'

'A team of officers led by Captain Kumalo swooped on David Plaistowe's home this morning and arrested him. My sources tell me it's for suspected money laundering. They also tell me he's wanted abroad for similar crimes. Care to comment?'

'Are you serious?' he asked with genuine surprise, at the same time recalling the information passed onto him by Snyman.

'Yes, I'm serious,' replied the reporter. 'I've been investigating Plaistowe for a long time and have to say this doesn't come as a surprise to me.'

'Well, it comes as a complete surprise to me,' he said. 'My word, who would've thought.'

'Any comment?' persisted the reporter. 'Either about the arrest or the Winters case?'

'Not on the arrest, and I can't talk about the other matter, at least not yet.'

'Okay, need to shoot, got a story to write.'

Julia slid out of bed and offered to make coffee. 'When I'm back you can tell me what the hell those phone calls were about.'

His vacant expression as he stared out of the window told her he hadn't heard a thing she had said. Once he had sorted his thoughts he dispatched a group WhatsApp message to the legal team, Jeremy and Lucy.

"It seems the P.I. was right. David Plaistowe arrested this morning by Kumalo for money laundering, here and abroad. That's all the info I have. Will be in touch when I know more."

Next he had to glean what he could from Kumalo. Gary was surprised that he took his call.

'You've no doubt heard, Mr Edwards. The arrest was the priority I mentioned to you. Maybe, perhaps maybe, you'll now accept no one has any hold on me.'

'All of us say things in the heat of the moment that we don't mean,' Gary replied. 'Is it true the arrest has nothing to do with Amanda Shelton's rape and murder?'

'That's true. It concerns other matters I've been working on for many months, and now I can tackle the leads you and Pillay have been banging on about.'

'Speaking about Pillay, I hope you've not fired him. He's a great policeman. All defence lawyers who've dealt with him will tell you so.'

'I know what you're getting at. No, I haven't fired him and I've no intention of firing him. As you said, all of us say things in the heat of the moment which we don't mean.'

'Thank you, Captain. It seems I've underestimated you. Please accept my apologies.'

'No apology is necessary. And so that you know, I haven't underestimated you. You are one helluva lawyer. Anyway, enough of this sentimental stuff, I've got work to do.'

Julia sat on the edge of the bed and passed him a steaming cup.

'What a strange world,' he said.

She waited, but he didn't offer any explanation. 'What are you waiting for?' she asked. 'Put some clothes on and tell me about this strange world.'

'I will, but give me a minute, I need to make a quick call and then I'm all yours.'

'Is that a promise?' she asked, touching his bare chest.

He smiled and winked at her, at the same time bringing the phone to his ear. 'Dhanraj, I've heard the news and spoken to Captain Kumalo. I know you guys will be flat out so two quick points. First, Kumalo thinks you're a great cop and has no intention of firing you. And second, forget what I said about Kumalo the last time we spoke. I now know he got close to Plaistowe to infiltrate what he's been up to.'

'He was pretty smart about that,' said Pillay. 'None of us in the office had any idea. Let's catch up later, I'm drowning here.'

He switched his phone to silent and lay down next to Julia. 'Right, let me tell you what's been happening,' he said giving her a soft kiss on the cheek.

'Tell me later,' she replied, snuggling into him.

After surfacing from the bedroom, he sent out another WhatsApp message, this time to Elaine Shelton and Lucy.

"Hi Elaine. By now you would've heard the news, I'm sure, about David Plaistowe's arrest. Since we were last in touch there have been some extraordinary

218

developments bringing us closer to finding Amanda's attacker. When convenient it would be appreciated if Lucy and I could meet with you and your husband to update you."

As the day progressed, he received more and more information from various sources about Plaistowe's money laundering activities. It wasn't surprising, given his elevated profile, that his arrest dominated airtime on all the South African news channels. By late afternoon some of the international news agencies were also carrying the story.

Gary kept the legal team appraised as new information came to light, and asked Jeremy and Lucy to come to his home as soon as the rush-hour traffic dissipated.

They arrived in time as the perfect evening became more special as the sun dipped towards the western horizon, splashing the sky in a warm red glow. The fragrant garden permeated the air, and the quieting birdsong could be heard above the burbling water trickling over the rocks into the pool.

Gary poured the drinks and then, suddenly, the bird chatter was gone. He told them about the events of the day, including Kumalo's promise to move forward on the investigation.

'What's he going to do?' asked Jeremy.

'Unless Kumalo's kidding me, which I'm reasonably confident he isn't, I believe we'll see a forensic sweep of David's Bentley plus an analysis of tracker and mobile phone information to plot the precise movements of the Plaistowes and Bagley-Smith. We'll probably see an interrogation by the police of these three gentlemen and, now that David has been arrested, perhaps an interview with Carol Ibbets.'

'What do you think will be the outcome?' asked Jeremy.

'Hopefully you'll be exonerated, and the police will find Amanda's killer,' said Gary.

Their conversation turned to the charges against David Plaistowe. 'From what I hear,' said Gary, 'hundreds of millions of dollars are involved in at least five countries.'

Three days later Kumalo invited Gary to a meeting at his office. The detective got straight into it in businesslike fashion without demonstrating any of the arrogance and rudeness of their past interactions.

'We've analysed information from Plaistowe senior's tracker company, and from the phone service providers of both Plaistowes and Bagley-Smith.'

'That was pretty quick,' said Gary. 'I'm all ears.'

'Bagley-Smith's story checks out.'

'Really,' replied Gary with surprise. 'He was high on my list of suspects.'

'I've learned over the years, and again recently, things aren't always what they seem to be. I think you're going to find the next bit interesting. David Plaistowe's Bentley left the hotel at six minutes past two on the Sunday morning. Both he and his son were in the car as confirmed by the hotel's CCTV footage and registers. According to Plaistowe junior's phone records his mobile remained static at the hotel until about noon on the Sunday when, as verified again by the hotel records, he collected his car.'

'Okay, got that,' said Gary. 'Roger and his father leave the hotel without Roger's phone. Where do they go?'

'Brace yourself, Mr Edwards.'

He held his breath.

'Amanda Shelton's cottage.'

22

Kumalo and Pillay pulled up to the ostentatious gates at David Plaistowe's home on Westcliff Ridge. This would be the first time they had been in touch with Plaistowe since his release on bail a few days prior. Kumalo surveyed the location, letting out a soft whistle. 'What an unbelievable view. I've not seen anything like it.'

Pillay announced their arrival on the intercom to a member of the domestic staff.

Fifteen minutes later, Plaistowe came on the line. 'What do you want? You know full well I've nothing to say on the ridiculous charges you've trumped up against me.'

'We're here on something totally different,' said Kumalo in a gravelly tone. 'Let us in.'

Although reluctant, Plaistowe eventually relented when Kumalo threatened him with arrest. He led the police officers to a sheltered area near the tennis court, out of earshot of his wife and staff.

'Now, what's it this time? More silly allegations?'

'We're here to ask you some questions about the Amanda Shelton case,' said Kumalo.

'I've already given you a statement so stop wasting my time. Does the National Commissioner of Police know about this visit?'

'Look, Mr Plaistowe, we can do this the easy way here at your home, or we can take you down to the station and do it there,' replied Kumalo in a clipped voice. 'You decide.'

'Get on with it.'

'Very well, I'll get straight to the point. According to your previous statement to us, and your separate statement to Advocate Dlamini, on the night of Amanda Shelton's death you gave your son a lift to his apartment in Melrose Arch and then returned to the hotel to collect your mobile, whereafter you drove here, to your home.'

Plaistowe was about to respond but Kumalo cut him short.

'Let me finish and then I'll give you a chance. You stated quite categorically that you didn't travel north of Sandton City because there was no need. Here's the difficulty we have with those statements. Records and data from your mobile service provider and your car tracker service show you went from the hotel, with Roger in the car, to Amanda Shelton's cottage in Rivonia, remaining there for nearly twenty minutes before returning to the hotel. The records and data from the hotel show that you spent fourteen minutes in the hotel. And then street cameras have you travelling to Melrose Arch and then to your home. You've lied about the trips, you've lied about not going to Rivonia, and you've lied about leaving your mobile in the hotel. Why the lies, and what were you doing at the cottage?'

Plaistowe's usual ruddy complexion faded rapidly and his shoulders slumped.

'Before you answer, if you choose to answer, Mr Plaistowe, Detective Sergeant Pillay here is going to remind you of your constitutional—'

'Don't waste time, I know my rights.'

Ignoring Plaistowe, Pillay informed him of his rights.

Plaistowe elected to remain silent.

'One more thing, Mr Plaistowe,' said Kumalo, 'we're impounding your Bentley for forensic examination.'

Less than an hour later Gary declined Kumalo's call, not wanting to interrupt his meeting with the Sheltons. Mr Shelton understood the reasons for initially being kept out of the picture, confirming he would have confronted Kumalo had he been briefed on their investigations.

'I'm sorry your friend has had to endure the accusations and humiliation,' he said.

'It won't be long now before justice is done,' replied Gary as he and Lucy rose, ready to leave. 'I know it will never bring your daughter back.' He stepped towards the Sheltons, enveloping them both in his huge arms. 'We'll be in touch.'

Lucy invited him in for a drink when he dropped her off at her apartment. 'Next time, Lucy. Julia's probably already at my place. I promised to cook her supper.'

'This is becoming serious,' she said, leaning against the passenger door.

He smiled and waved as he drove off.

'Gary, quick, come and see,' shouted Julia from the lounge. 'Some news about David Plaistowe.'

"Some breaking news... David Plaistowe, one of the country's leading lawyers and chairperson of the largest law firm in Africa, and a director of many public companies, died from a gunshot wound earlier

this evening at his Westcliff home. We have no other details at this time."

Gary called Kumalo. 'Have you seen the news, Mr Edwards?'

'I have, a few seconds ago. What happened?'

The officer told him about the visit to Plaistowe's home earlier that day and the impounding of the Bentley. 'I think it became too much for him,' he said. 'We'll have to wait and see whether he left a suicide note.'

Gary declined the many incoming calls so he could finish his conversation with Kumalo. 'Have you confronted Roger yet?' he asked.

'We were intending to do that tomorrow but given what's happened we'll leave it for a few days. We'll stay in touch.'

Julia had slipped off to the kitchen where he found her with apron already donned. 'Jules, that's not necessary. I said I would do supper.'

She grabbed his arm and planted a noisy kiss on his lips. 'There'll be many more chances, handsome. I know you're going to be busy tonight.'

He attended to some of the incoming calls. Surprisingly, one of the voice messages was from Carol Ibbets, asking Gary to call her back. He toyed with the thought of leaving it until the morning, but his instincts told him otherwise.

'Carol, you called. What a dreadful business.'

'Thanks for getting back to me so quickly,' she said.

'Yea, very unexpected. Do you know what happened?'

'The police are still investigating but it seems he shot himself. I can only surmise that it had become too much for him.'

'I've heard the police were at his home earlier this afternoon and took away one of his cars. What was that all about?' she asked.

"I'm afraid David seems to be implicated in Amanda's death. His car's been impounded for forensic examination.'

Gary heard gasps on the line. A long silence followed before she said that she intended returning to Canada. 'I've been thinking about this for a while, it's time.'

'When?'

'Soon. I have to give two weeks' notice at work.'

'Given what's happened, won't you now tell me whose voice you heard in the hotel basement? It couldn't have been David because CCTV footage shows he hadn't gone down there by that time.'

Another long delay followed before she replied. 'Let me think about it.'

'Please. You know it's the right thing to do. The fear you had about upsetting your father is no longer relevant because of what the police already know and because of David's passing. Justice must be done, and a young man needs to get his life back.'

Gary felt the excitement building as he approached the offices of the Johannesburg Murder and Robbery Squad; this time round as the guest of Captain Kumalo. Gary had doubts about the propriety of attending the questioning, but, what the hell, Kumalo was a big boy who could look after himself, and Gary could see no prejudice to Jeremy. True to his word, Kumalo had waited a few days before bringing Roger in for interrogation.

Gary, not visible to those inside the interrogation room, watched and listened to Roger ignore his attorney's counsel to remain silent, and instead putting on a show of cocky confidence. He leaned back in his chair and looked everywhere except at Kumalo and Pillay.

'Ask me what you like, I've nothing to hide,' he blustered.

'On the night in question, when you were in the hotel basement, before going to look for a lift home, did you hear or see either Jeremy Winters or Amanda Shelton?' asked Kumalo.

'As I told you before in my statement, no.'

'Tell us where you and your father went after you both left the hotel in the early hours of that Sunday morning?'

'He took me home to Melrose Arch.'

'Going south along Oxford Road and then east past Wanderers cricket stadium?' asked Pillay.

'Exactly.'

'Did you go anywhere north of Sandton City, towards Rivonia?' asked Pillay.

'No need to, my apartment's south-east of Sandton City.'

'Are you certain?' interjected Kumalo.

Roger shuffled in his chair, looked around the room and then at his attorney, before responding with a provocative question. 'Are you asking whether I'm certain about where my apartment is or about not going towards Rivonia?'

'Don't be silly, Mr Plaistowe, you know what we mean,' said Pillay in an admonishing tone.

'I'm certain on both counts,' said Roger spitting out the words.

Kumalo swivelled his chair through a wide arc, giving Roger and the attorney his back. He paused before alighting and heading across the small room where he leaned against the wall, facing Plaistowe.

'Here's the problem we have with your story. We have proof of the Bentley leaving the hotel with the two of you in the car, and then travelling north along Rivonia Road in the opposite direction you say you went.'

226

'That's rubbish,' shouted Roger. 'I didn't go on Rivonia Road.'

Kumalo returned to his chair. 'Tell him what proof we have, Detective Sergeant Pillay, tell him.'

After Pillay did as he was told, Kumalo continued. 'In your previous statement to us you said that after finding your father at the party you both returned to the fifth basement so you could retrieve your wallet from your car. Why didn't you also take your mobile from the car?'

'I think I did,' said a more subdued Roger.

'No, you didn't,' snapped Kumalo. 'We can show with records and data from your service provider that your phone didn't leave the hotel until noon on the Sunday.'

'Perhaps I'm mistaken,' he replied. 'I was drunk, you know.'

'Is that why you don't remember travelling on Rivonia Road with your father?' asked Pillay.

Roger shifted again in his chair, looking at his attorney often but avoiding eye contact with the police officers. 'I've already told you I didn't travel on Rivonia Road.' He leaned over to his attorney and whispered into his ear.

'Can we have a short break?' asked the attorney. 'My client wants to consult me.'

Kumalo gestured to Pillay who escorted them to another room down the passage. Kumalo looked in the direction of the viewing room, smiled and drew his index finger across his throat. Gary smiled even though he knew Kumalo couldn't see him.

After returning, Roger said he wanted to clarify something. 'I haven't been frank with you about the Rivonia journey. I was trying to protect my father. I did start the trip with him but shortly after leaving the hotel I asked him to let me out of the car. I found a taxi to take me home.'

Kumalo burst out laughing before turning serious once more. 'Is this another one of your lies, Mr Plaistowe? Why didn't you mention this before?'

'I was embarrassed and wanted to protect my father.'

'We're listening,' replied the senior detective, rolling his eyes.

'As soon as we left the hotel my father said he would take me home after visiting a club he liked in Rivonia. It's a discreet brothel for elite clients. We had a heated exchange as I didn't approve and, in any event, I wanted to get home.'

'How can you talk like that about your late father?' came the retort from Kumalo.

'You left me no choice, I take no joy speaking about this, but the truth has to come out.'

The police officers withheld any further information they had about the trips, including the stopover at Amanda's cottage, deciding to confront Roger with that at another time.

'Do you still have the clothes you wore to the party?' asked Kumalo.

'Of course.'

'I'm suspending this interview now so you, your attorney and Sergeant Pillay can go to your apartment where you will hand over to Pillay the clothes you wore. Don't worry about the underwear or socks; we won't be needing those.'

Roger shot his attorney a perplexed look as they left the room with Pillay leading the way.

'Well, how do you think that went?' Kumalo asked Gary when he fetched him from the viewing room.

'He's lying through his teeth,' said Gary. 'Plaistowe senior may not have been a paragon of virtue but visit a brothel in the presence of his son? Nah, I don't buy that. Where to from here?'

'We'll send his clothes to the forensic guys examining the Bentley and see what comes up. Hopefully something will. I'm worried we don't have enough to prove the Plaistowes were the perpetrators. I need something more concrete.'

Gary knew there was a serious risk that Roger Plaistowe could get away with the crime. Even though the circumstances surrounding David Plaistowe's lies and his visit to Amanda's cottage would move the spotlight even further away from Jeremy, Gary remained concerned that many would still wonder whether he killed Amanda. In desperation he called Carol Ibbets.

23

Early the following morning Gary, Lucy and Carol jogged out of Zoo Lake carpark. Before Gary could tell Carol about Roger's interrogation, she stopped abruptly.

'The firm's agreed to release me early,' she said. 'I leave for Canada the day after tomorrow.'

Gary and Lucy looked at each other, astonished by the accelerated plans. 'What's the rush, why so soon?' asked Lucy.

'All this is too much, I want to get back where I belong.'

They resumed their run and Gary updated Carol on the interrogation, deliberately sparing no detail. 'Roger lied and when caught out he invented a story about his father wanting to visit a brothel and him taking a taxi home.'

Carol didn't respond, appearing anxious as she chewed at a fingernail.

Gary knew he wouldn't have another opportunity to persuade her to open up. 'All the signs point to Roger and his father being involved in Amanda's death, but the police need more, Amanda's parents need more, and Jeremy needs more. Before you leave, I implore you to do the right thing. Please, Carol, I beg you. Think of the Sheltons and think of Jeremy and think of your own peace of mind.'

Instead of replying, Carol picked up the pace, pulling Gary and Lucy along, up the incline past the zoo. Their breathing quickened until they crested the hill and were able to jog more comfortably.

'I should've spoken out when Lucy first asked me,' she said almost inaudibly. 'I'm sorry. Please tell the Sheltons and Jeremy I'm terribly sorry.' She stopped again, wiping at her eyes with the bottom of her running vest.

'I know who shouted at Amanda. I can never forget those chilling words. "You've just fucked him in his car. Am I not good enough for you? Is that it? Answer me, is that it, you bloody whore?" I so regret not acting; I could've saved her life. But I was, still am, scared of him.'

'Why?' asked Lucy.

'He took me out on a date once and when I refused to sleep with him, he became quite physical.' She paused. 'And then he threatened me with all sorts of nasty things, reminding me who his father was.'

'So, it was Roger,' commented Gary.

'Yes,' she said, letting out a sigh.

'Thank you, Carol, thank you. This confirms what much of the evidence points to.'

Lucy hugged her. 'You're a courageous and decent human being.'

'Because of you, justice will be done,' said Gary.

She agreed to accompany them to Kumalo's office later that day to make a formal statement, and agreed to return to South Africa if needed to give evidence.

A week later Pillay invited Gary to witness another interrogation session with Roger Plaistowe. The new suspect was again accompanied by his attorney; Gary watched from the viewing room. After being read his constitutional rights, Kumalo got stuck in.

'I'm going to tell you what evidence we have against you, Mr Plaistowe, and then ask you to comment, unless of course you choose not to. You told us last time that shortly after leaving the hotel you and your father had a fallout and you left his car to take a taxi home. However, your father's tracker and mobile phone data show that after the car left the hotel it didn't stop, not even at traffic lights, until it reached Amanda Shelton's cottage. So you must've been in the car when it reached the cottage.'

Plaistowe's attorney glanced at him with a furrowed brow.

Kumalo, not pausing for any response, pressed on. 'After about twenty minutes the car left the cottage and returned to the hotel. We believe you and Amanda were hidden in the boot and that's why only your father is seen on the CCTV footage at that time.'

'That's sheer horse shit,' shouted Roger. 'I was never in the boot.'

'Well, we have the forensic results back, and they tell an interesting tale. Carpet fibres from the boot of the car were found on the trousers you wore to the party, and on the side of Amanda's dress. And that's not all. Fibres from a carpet in the cottage were found on the back of that dress and in the boot of the Bentley. And a blood stain in the boot came from Amanda.'

Kumalo glimpsed at the viewing room window. Gary could swear he saw the twitching of the lip.

'And how do you think those fibres and the blood stain got there,' asked Kumalo rhetorically. 'I'll tell you how. From you and Amanda being in the boot. She must've been unconscious or maybe even dead for you and your father to bring her back to the basement where her body was found.'

Kumalo began to strut around the room, both hands tucked into the front pockets of his jeans.

'I hope you can see where this is going,' said Kumalo, stopping for a moment and looking down at Roger. 'After some fourteen minutes back at the hotel, the Bentley left, and the CCTV footage shows only your father in the car. But after about four hundred metres, the street cameras along Oxford Road show a passenger in the front seat. We believe, Mr Plaistowe, that you again hid in the boot until you were clear of the hotel's cameras and then you jumped into the front seat. Other street cameras, as well as tracker and mobile phone data, show that your father drove to Melrose Arch, stopped briefly at your apartment block and then returned to Oxford Road before heading to his home in Westcliff.'

The small muscles along Roger's jaw tightened and he began to wring his hands, glancing at his attorney, and gesturing as if wanting to say something and then backing off.

'On top of all this overwhelming evidence, Mr Plaistowe,' said Kumalo, now on a roll, 'we also have a witness who heard you shouting at Amanda in the basement at about one that morning, some thirty minutes before you go looking for your father. I'm going to read what she heard you shout.'

Armed with Carol's statement, he read: '"You've just fucked him in his car. Am I not good enough for you? Is that it? Answer me, is that it, you bloody whore?"' Kumalo read it again and again and again. Roger's head slumped onto his chest as he brought both hands to the top of his head.

'That's quite enough,' said his attorney, 'you're abusing my client.'

Kumalo ignored him. 'We believe, Mr Plaistowe, that you spied on Jeremy Winters and Amanda having sex and when she got out of the car, you came on to her, and when she refused your advances, you abused her verbally. You then knocked her unconscious with a champagne bottle and raped her.'

There was a deathly hush in the room except for the noisy flickering light above the interrogation desk. Kumalo's stern look needed no words. Pillay peered at him and shrugged.

'And here is the last bit before I'm done,' said Kumalo. 'After attacking Amanda, you realised the horrific enormity of your assault and went running to your father for help. The two of you returned to the scene to find her gone. You concluded, I believe, that she had returned to her home. You both went there, no doubt to reason with her and when that failed, one of you strangled her. You returned her body to the scene in the hope that Winters would be blamed.'

An uncomfortably long pause followed as both officers waited for a response from their suspect. They were disappointed.

'What do you have to say about all that, Mr Plaistowe?' asked Kumalo with a sneer.

Gary was impressed. Kumalo and Pillay had played a good hand.

Plaistowe whispered to his attorney who then addressed the police officers. 'My client is exercising his constitutional right to remain silent.'

At Kumalo's nudging, Pillay stepped forward and placed his right hand on Plaistowe's left shoulder. 'Mr Plaistowe, I'm arresting you on charges of raping and murdering Amanda Shelton in the early hours of

Sunday morning 8 December 2019. Please stand up, turn around and put both hands behind your back.'

As the cuffs locked onto Plaistowe's wrists, Gary fired off a group WhatsApp to the legal team, Jeremy and his parents.

"At last, Roger Plaistowe arrested for raping and murdering Amanda. Will follow up later with details."

As he finished dispatching a similar WhatsApp to Carol, Kumalo entered the viewing room. The officer extended his right hand and as Gary reciprocated, Kumalo instead hugged him. 'Well done and thank you, Mr Edwards, you should be proud. If ever I need a lawyer, you're my man.'

'That's decent of you to say so, Captain Kumalo, and well done to you and Sergeant Pillay. I suspect it won't be long before all the news channels sing your praises. I can already see the headlines: "Top cop breaks international money laundering syndicate and cracks Egoli Hotel murder case."'

'Stop your B.S.,' said Kumalo laughingly, slapping Gary playfully on the back.

'I know Ashley Dobson from *The Chronicle* has been investigating Plaistowe's offshore shenanigans for years and she's been all over this Egoli case. Look out for her column,' said Gary.

Kumalo smiled as he led Gary down the passage to his office. 'I have a bottle of something special which I've been saving for a special occasion. It's time to break the seal.'

The detective opened a bottle of Johnnie Walker Blue Label and poured a generous tot into each of two tumblers.

'To us,' he said, before taking a swig. Gary echoed his words. Kumalo lifted his glass again. 'To Jeremy Winters, and to the Sheltons, and to my right-hand man, Detective Sergeant Pillay.' He took another gulp as Gary joined in the toast.

'Now it's my turn,' said Gary as Kumalo topped up their glasses. He stood and lifted his tumbler to Kumalo, 'To one helluva detective.'

They both drained their glasses.

There it was again, the twitching upper lip, this time revealing something close to satisfaction.

'Any sign of a suicide note from Plaistowe senior?' asked Gary.

'Nothing, but it's clear from the evidence that he shot himself.'

Kumalo offered his guest a refill.

'I'd love to but I need to visit the Sheltons with the good news. Maybe some other time.'

'Sure, but before you go, I have two questions. How the hell did you notice the dresses had been switched, and why do you think they were switched?'

'My P.A. was the one who first noticed the change when we pored over the police photographs. She and Amanda had gone shopping together on the Saturday of the party and she remembered the dresses Amanda had bought.'

'And my second question?'

'The evidence at the cottage showed Amanda had a shower when she got home, put on her gown and dumped the halter neck dress in the wastebin. After the Plaistowes killed her or rendered her unconscious they decided to return her body, re-clothed in her party dress, to the fifth basement to stage the murder scene. Not realising the original dress had been discarded, they grabbed the wrong dress out of the closet. After they dressed her, probably as she lay on the floor, the dress picked up some fibres from the carpet. I can't think of any other explanation.'

'Interesting,' said Kumalo. 'That sounds feasible.'

On his way to the Winters' home, after spending time with the Sheltons, Gary pulled off the road to send a voice mail to *The Chronicle* reporter.

'Gary Edwards here. Roger Plaistowe was arrested a couple of hours ago on charges of raping and murdering Amanda Shelton. If you still want to chat, let me know. I'm going to be tied up for the rest of the day.'

As Gary parked the Ferrari next to Lucy's car, Jeremy came running along the cobbled path, punching the air repeatedly with a clenched fist. His folks followed closely behind with Lucy. As huge as he was, Gary managed to remove himself quickly from the sports car to congratulate his friend. 'Thank you, thank you, Gary, my dearest friend. You believed me, you fought for me, and we won.'

His parents and Lucy didn't conceal their emotions either, extolling Gary's commitment and sacrifices.

'Hey, guys, I love all this fuss, but without all your efforts, support and love it wouldn't have been possible. And Jeremy, I salute you especially, for your sheer guts, fortitude and determination in weathering this terrible, terrible storm.'

Before they sat down, Mr Winters appeared with the bottle of champagne he had been saving. He popped the cork. 'This day has been a long time coming.'

In the middle of the toasts, Gary's phone buzzed. He excused himself, mouthing to the others that it was Captain Kumalo. When he returned after the call, he saw the anxiety plastered over their faces. 'Relax, relax. Roger Plaistowe has signed a full confession.'

According to Kumalo the confession confirmed the version of events with which Roger was confronted during his interrogation. He admitted that he and his father tried to buy Amanda off and when she refused and threatened to lay a charge of rape against him, he strangled her.

After Gary shared the details of Roger's interrogation, from which the Winters and Lucy derived immense satisfaction, Jeremy asked about the next step.

'Well, you'll need to appear in the High Court so the charges can be formally withdrawn,' said Gary. 'I'll phone the prosecutor later and see if we can get this done in the next few days.'

'But what about Jeremy's reputation?' asked Mrs Winters. 'His good name has been dragged through the mud.'

'Believe me, the bad publicity surrounding the Plaistowe family right now will take care of that. Jeremy's reputation will be completely restored.'

'But shouldn't Jeremy be suing someone?' she asked.

'Mom, Gary's right. When the media is done with the story, there is no way that a single person will think I harmed Amanda.'

'You've suffered so much my son; you were on the brink of a breakdown. Shouldn't you be compensated?'

'Mom, let it go. I'm not going to drag this out any longer. Even if I wanted to sue the police, I'd probably lose. They had enough circumstantial evidence to suspect me. I guess I could go against the Plaistowes, but I want nothing more to do with that lot.'

Although Jeremy had longed for this day, his nerves got the better of him as he waited anxiously in the dock. His eyes swept over the public gallery packed with friends and colleagues and then to the dark wood panelling and the portraits of judges from bygone eras. He peered up at the clock and saw the time edging towards 11 a.m.

Mr Justice Shamsi entered and quickly disposed of some unrelated formalities. The prosecutor, still standing, wasted no time. 'My Lord, I appear for the State in this matter, and my learned friend, Mr Dlamini, appears for Jeremy Winters, the accused.'

Advocate Dlamini stood and bowed as was customary, before resuming his seat.

'My Lord,' said the prosecutor, 'the State withdraws the charges against Mr Winters, who was framed by two unscrupulous criminals. He is innocent.'

'Stand up, Mr Winters,' said the judge. 'As the State has withdrawn all charges against you, you are free to go.'

The courtroom erupted with applause and cheering as the tail end of the judicial gown disappeared hastily through the door behind the bench.

After an abstemious lunch with the Winters family, Lucy and the rest of the legal team, Gary pulled up at the security gate when the guard waved him down. 'This came for you, sir,' he said, handing over a large parcel which barely fitted onto the passenger seat.

'Who is it from?' asked Gary.

'I don't know, sir, it came with a courier about an hour ago.'

He was not expecting a delivery from anyone, and reasoned that the package must contain the early proof signage for the new law firm. He felt the excitement rise within himself at the thought of Edwards and Winters Incorporated, and of Lucy taking on the management role.

He set the parcel down on the carpeted floor of the lounge, leaning it against one of the couches, and decided to review the proofs later. After turning on some light classical music, he poured a double gin and tonic before collapsing on the recliner. He closed his eyes, letting his mind drift over the events of the last four months, the closing of an old chapter and the prospect of new beginnings, about his growing love for Julia, and about the gaping hole in his life left by the death of Charlie.

By the time he woke it was late afternoon. He wiped the sleep from his eyes, stretching as he rose from the comfort of the chair. *Let's have a look at these proofs; hopefully they've got it right this time.* He grabbed a pair of scissors from the kitchen and commenced removing the wrapping, layer by layer, failing to understand why so much bubble wrap had been used.

Finally, the last layer slipped to the floor and Charlie emerged in his full magnificence from the depths of an oil painting. Gary took in every detail and every nuance as if Charlie was still alive, sitting on his favourite chair, basking in the sun. The engraved plate at the bottom of the frame read "CHARLIE". Gary noticed the familiar signature in the bottom right corner as that of the well-known artist Gordon Kingley. When Gary's shaking hands managed to open the accompanying envelope, he wiped at his eyes with the back of his wrist, bringing the message on the card into focus:

"With indescribable gratitude, deep respect, and unending love. The Winters."

THE END